From 14-year-old Nancy's diary:

I'M IN A NIGHTMARE ...
I'm going to wake up any minute now. I've got
to. I can see Doctor Miller's face with his eyes
all glazed up, and Mom looking like she's a
marble statue. We can sense something is really
wrong when Doctor Miller keeps telling us how
great we are, like he can't really get out what he
wants to say. Then he slowly tells me that my
blood samples have come back, and I have ...
the HIV virus! His mouth keeps moving, but I
can't hear words anymore. I can't feel; I can't
think. From far off in the distance, I can hear
myself sobbing.

I've got to face it ... I'm not going to have a
career, or a husband or a family. My heart is
bursting. I AM GOING TO DIE ...

"IT HAPPENED TO NANCY may well be one
of the most important books published for this
generation of teenagers and their parents."
Caroline Tanner,
School Counselor

It happened to Nancy

by an ANONYMOUS TEENAGER
EDITED BY BEATRICE SPARKS, Ph.D.

AN AVON FLARE BOOK

This is a work of nonfiction. It is based on the actual diary of a teenage girl who was infected with the AIDS virus as a result of date-rape. It is a highly personal and specific chronicle, and, as such, we hope it will provide insights into the increasingly complicated world in which we live. Names and places have been changed at the request of "Nancy's" parents.

AVON BOOKS, INC.
1350 Avenue of the Americas
New York, New York 10019

Copyright © 1994 by Beatrice M. Sparks
Published by arrangement with the editor
Library of Congress Catalog Card Number: 93-90637
ISBN: 0-380-77315-5
www.avonbooks.com

First Avon Flare Printing: March 1994

AVON FLARE TRADEMARK REG. U.S. PAT. OFF. AND IN OTHER COUNTRIES, MARCA REGISTRADA. HECHO EN U.S.A.

Printed in the U.S.A.

30 29

NANCY'S DEDICATION

Dedicated to every kid
who thinks AIDS can't happen
to him or her

It Happened to Nancy is a book
that all parents and kids should read:

"Only when one has been intimately involved with a real AIDS-infected person like Nancy can one slightly comprehend the overwhelmingness of the disease."

Milton Norbaum, M.D.
AIDS Specialist

"*It Happened to Nancy* is a deeply disturbing book because it faces AIDS honestly, realistically and head-on.
Up to 30 percent of people who have AIDS are diagnosed in their twenties, which means most were infected in their teens."

Dorean Hadley Staudacher
Psychiatrist working with AIDS

". . . the scary thing is that Nancy could be someone you don't know you know."

Teenage Male Reader

NOTE

Names and places have been changed at the request of Nancy's parents.

"We are trying to keep our precious Nancy with the laughing eyes in our hearts and minds exactly as she was during her happy, excited, nothing-can-stop-me, invincible life, *before* HIV-AIDS. However, common sense tells us that cannot be. Therefore, we share Nancy's difficult times as well as her joyous times with you, hoping that her experiences will educate and enlighten adults and perhaps safeguard some young people. That was her deepest and most sincere wish!"

FOREWORD

Precious little fourteen-year-old Nancy's tragic battle with AIDS becomes all the more tragic because of her extremely lowered natural immune system, which allowed the virus to so quickly ravage her delicate body. Ordinarily the latency period from infection to symptoms for AIDS is considered to be from five to ten years.

The World Health Organization (WHO) estimates that, to date, "at least 10 to 12 million adults have been infected with HIV." I worry about all the beautiful, innocent young Nancys.

Dr. Dathan Sheranian
(one of Nancy's doctors)

It happened to Nancy

Saturday, April 14

8:01 A.M.

I can't believe it. Tonight's the night I've been waiting for forever. At least it seems like forever since February 10, when El's Aunt Pauline picked up the tickets. Imagine *me* going to a concert. A Garth Brooks concert! A few months ago El and Red and Dorie and I whined and nagged and groaned and moaned because we weren't allowed to go to the U2 concert. Now we're going to see Garth! Garth! I heard on television that he's loud-loud-loud and that he jumps off a high platform, grabs a rope and swings high out over the audience, with strobe lights flashing in all different colors and everything looking sort of smoky. Plus all sorts of other wild, woolly and wacky stuff. It's going to be almost like going to a *real* rock concert, which, boo-hoo, none of our mothers will allow us to attend.

6:45 P.M.

Oh chips, isn't it strange how slowly time goes by when you want it to go fast and how fast it goes when you want it to go slow? Anyway . . . for now . . . life is great! . . . it's good! . . . it's wonderful! . . . it's fun! . . . it's fab! . . . it's sunshiny inside!—and *why* don't they come? Why, why, WHY? WHY don't they hurry up and pick me up? I've tried on everything in my closet, plus every combination of everything in my closet, and I've redone my hair 97½ times.

Oops, there's the doorbell. My chariot and my friends have arrived. I, Cinderella, am off to the ball.

2 A.M.

It's 2 A.M., and I can't sleep. I don't think I'll ever sleep again. I can't believe what happened tonight. It was like a movie, only better and louder and more exciting than any movie could ever be! Red and El and Dorie and I walking into the concert auditorium trying to look like we weren't excited! So excited that we could hardly keep from jumping up and down and squealing!! We were also pretending Aunt Pauline wasn't with us. And grown-uply endeavoring not to giggle—but *that was impossible!* There was so much excitement in the air that you couldn't help *feel* it. I mean *REALLY* feel it, like it was crunchy fall leaves or soft cloth or something . . . maybe solid but squishy or gauzy and wispy and changing, ever changing, like a planet or galaxy weaving through space.

When the strobe lights turned on, they flashed absolutely through my body. We were sitting next to a big speaker, and the music pierced every molecule in me. It was mag! Really magnif! I was part of it, and it was part of me, a new dimension!

Then, uggggg, about halfway through the concert a couple of rednecks came in and tried to sit in front of us. They said those were their seats. The people sitting there said they weren't. A scuffle started. Almost immediately cops appeared from nowhere and literally surrounded the area. Aunt Pauline tried to herd El and Red and Dorie and me away from the confusion, but, wouldn't you know it, I fell down. For a moment I was panic-stricken because people were almost walking on me, and someone grabbed my purse. Then I didn't even care about that. I just wanted to crawl out of there alive. When I finally got out of the line of fire, I tried to get the attention of a policeman to tell him about my purse, but they were either trying to get people to sit down as they dragged the two nutsos away, or they were trying to get back to their own posts.

Amazingly, most of the auditorium wasn't even aware that there was a problem—they kept it so isolated. I leaned against a post, trying to become invisible, because I had started to have an asthma attack. I was so terrorized I couldn't breathe, and I was *alone!* More alone in those thousands of people than I had ever been in my life. I was hyperventilating and about to pass out, and no one seemed to care. They didn't want me, or anything else, for that matter, to interfere with their wild and woolly enjoyment.

Just as I was beginning to feel the blackness dragging me completely under, I sensed a soft hand on my shoulder and a gentle voice whispering in my ear, "Relax, relax. I'll get you out into the center hall, where you can sit down and get some air . . . shh . . . relax . . . relax. You'll be all right. . . . I'll take care of you."

He put his arm around my waist, and we walked down, down, down, down the endless rows of stairs. It hadn't seemed like there were nearly as many when we came up.

By the time we got out into the foyer, I felt better.

My hysterical terror was being replaced by a calm peace. The guy said he was Collin Eagle. He sat me on a bench and brought me a Coke, then began softly rubbing my back and quietly telling me to "relax . . . relax" . . . and I did! How could I not with his soft voice and his positive presence?

We moved over by the fountain, and it was nice. The music from the concert drifted out to us, and the dripping and the splashing of the water seemed to take over the melody line.

Collin and I talked like we had known each other forever, and I, who have always felt uneasy with boys, felt completely comfortable and comforted.

How could I have felt any other way? He had saved me.

We talked for a long time, waiting for Aunt Pauline to come down. Collin said she eventually had to come into the main hall looking for me.

Collin confided in me that he had a sister, Betsy Mae, who had asthma also; that's how he'd known what to do. He said he'd done for me exactly what he would have wanted someone to do for Betsy Mae if, God forbid, something like this ever happened to her.

We talked about how much we both loved South Carolina and joked about how the South was different from any other place on earth; about grits and red gravy and sweet potato pie and collard greens, which neither one of us could stand. He was like the big protective brother I'd never had, but had always wished I had had!

He told me he was eighteen and a freshman at the university, that he lived on campus but couldn't afford to belong to a fraternity. He said he'd come to school on a full scholarship; then he shyly let it slip out that this first semester he's on the Dean's List. I was sooooooo impressed. It was great that he was a kind, good-hearted Samaritan and handsome as any human hunk I'd ever seen. To be a brain on top of all that was super impressive.

I told Collin how my parents were divorced and how I lived with my mom in South Carolina during the school months and with my dad in Arizona during the summers. I told him I loved my dad, but I didn't love Phoenix, where sometimes it got so hot that the roads seemed like sticky tar instead of asphalt, and some people had green gravel rocks in their front yards instead of grass.

Collin asked me more and more questions about my parents. He loved hearing about them because both his mom and dad were killed in a car crash just last year. I felt sooooo sorry for him, but he didn't want to talk about it anymore. He said it hurt too much.

Isn't life funny? I can't remember a fraction of what my teachers tell me in school or what my parents tell me ever, or what I read, but I can remember distinctly every words that dear, dear Collin said.

After we talked a while, Collin got worried about Aunt Pauline not coming to find me and went to the office to see what we should do. When he got back he seemed really concerned, because Aunt Pauline hadn't checked in with the office or any of the officers. I broke down and started to bawl like a baby, of course. It was embarrassing, but I couldn't help it. It's scary to be at a big concert in another part of town with no money to even call Mom or El's mom or somebody. Collin saved my life again. He was so sweet. He put his arm around me and patted my shoulder like fat Mrs. Gomez, my Spanish teacher, does, and said he'd be happy to take me home if I wanted him to. Did I ever want him to! I wanted him to become part of the rest of my life. Already he was almost like family.

Collin assured me that Aunt Pauline would be sure to call my house, and she'd be relieved to find I was home. *Relieved* was not quite the word! Aunt Pauline and Mom were as mad as wet cats when I got home. Aunt Pauline said she'd reported me to the office and the guards, and then they had sat in the crumby little ticket office for hours waiting for some word. I tried to apologize to Aunt Pauline and explain, but she just said coldly that she was glad I was home and safe and hung up.

Oh wow, I just looked at the clock, and it's almost 4 A.M. I'd better get some zzzzzs. I've got a million things to do tomorrow.

P.S. I'm sorry I ruined everybody's evening, but I wouldn't give up mine for anything in the world!! There had to be some misunderstanding somewhere; with so many people that probably happened a lot.

Sunday, April 15

9:40 P.M.

Went to Columbia with Mom on business. Wasted the whole day! Had car trouble on the way home.

Monday, April 16

3:50 P.M.

I thought I'd be dead today at school. I only had about two and half hours' sleep, but I'm more alert and alive than I've ever been. Collin called to see if I was okay, just before I ran out to take the bus. Mom started lecturing me about taking rides with strangers and all that rehashed garbage, but thank goodness I didn't have time for much of it. Actually, I know she's right, but this is different. I wish I could talk to her about it, but of course I never can. She always has to tell me how *she* feels instead of ever letting me tell her how *I* feel. Why can't parents understand that kids have feelings too and brains?

At school I wanted to tell Red and Dorie and El every single detail about what happened, but they had been so worried about me, I couldn't let them know I had been having a wonderful time while they were thinking about the worst things in the world that were happening to me, kidnapping . . . and killing . . . and ugggg. Geez, I'm so sorry, but at least we all agree that it really was an exciting night that we'll never forget and that we'll probably all bore our kids and our grandkids with, when they get old enough to go to concerts themselves.

I ran all the way from the bus to my house, because I knew Collin was going to call me. I just knew it! And sure enough, just minutes after I got in the door, the phone rang. *Collin!* It was so mag! He just wanted to know if I'd recovered from the shock and my asthma attack and everything. Oh, heart, stop fluttering and trying to pop out of my chest and fly away. Collin asked me to meet him in the park at the far west by the little lake where they're just finishing the new section at 5. He said he'd never met anyone as verbal and open as I am and as gentle and that I reminded him of his family, especially his sister, Betsy Mae, who has had to live with their grandma since their parents died in the car crash. He misses them sooooooo much. Poor, poor dear Collin. My mom and dad bug me a lot, but I don't know how I'd ever stand it if they both died. Collin needs me. If I can just give him a little comfort to replace that which he's lost, I'll feel so privileged.

I'll leave a note for Mom saying I'm going to the mall to pick up something for one of my classes. . . . Ummm, I'll tell her I might be a little late because we'll pick up a bite to eat. I hope so!

9:30 P.M.

Sweet, wonderful Collin, he's so lost and lonely here in a town where he hardly knows anybody. He says it's hard for him to talk to people, but that with us it's almost like we're both just thinking out loud.

We sat and threw rocks in the lake and picked buttercups and talked about everything under the sun. I think he knows almost as much about me as I know about myself. I hated to tell him that I was only fourteen, but he said he knew it anyway, because that's how old his sister is, and it's his very favorite, special age for "his girls"! Imagine him calling me *HIS GIRL,* putting me in a category with his very own sister! Isn't that the mag and magnif of all magnificents?

Oops, I've finished the last three months of my diary in the last few days. Guess I'll just use my new looseleaf. I don't want to forget or lose one precious thought about my right-now life!

Mom just called. She is working on selling a big, new 143-unit complex. She's so busy she hardly has any time for me at all, except to nag me about my room and the dishes and stuff—stupid things!! How much are *any* of them going to count in the overall of life?

Collin's time and attention are like cream to a

starving, scruffy little unimportant kitten—*me!!* Deep inside, I guess I know that both my parents love me and try to give me "quality time," but "quality" time can NEVER match real, real, REAL TIME, no matter what anybody says! I think Collin and I are both very lonely, lost creatures!

Tuesday, April 17

9:10 P.M.

I can't believe it. Today I was called into the office, and I went there with fear and trembling. Crazy things buzzing through my mind. What had I done? Did the whole school know about Collin? Did they think that we had . . . that because he was four years older than me that he would be just after—you know. I wouldn't let myself think about it. It was too disgusting and degrading, and un-Collin. I decided I wouldn't let them say one bad thing about him! I'd drop out of school and go to Arizona with my dad first! Miracle of miracles, the desk girl just handed me a plain brown-paper-wrapped box. Shaking, I ran into the girl's room to open it. At first I was scared, because, like on television, I thought it might be something sinister or menacing, but it wasn't. Oh no, no, it wasn't at all! It was the most mag thing that had ever happened in all my life. Be still, my heart. A single white daisy lay in the bottom of the little box with a scribbled note: "In celebration of the third-day anniversary of the most precious day in my life, Your White Knight, I hope." It wasn't signed. It didn't need to be.

I was crying so hard that someone reported me to the counselor, and she suggested I go home. She had no idea that I was just unraveled with joy. I wish I had some way to get in touch with Collin, but he doesn't have a phone in his room. He has to use the pay phone in the hall. I guess I'll have to wait . . . but I can't . . . I can't . . . I can't . . . I'll pop.

Dear Collin. You are my dearest confidant, my valiant hero, my trusted friend, my future! *Literally* my happy, happy, forever future!!!

Friday, April 20

Time? What is mere time to me now?

I met Collin again today after school. In fact, I didn't even come home first. He called me really late last night and asked me to. He said he'd called twice, and Mom had answered, and he'd hung up because he was too shy to talk to her, and she might think some crazy thing, and she probably would. There is no way she can understand how much we can communicate with each other—how good we are for each other.

Collin doesn't talk too much about himself. He just likes to hear about me, and he likes to live through my mom and dad, his folks being dead and everything. I love to tell him. In fact, I think I'm getting closer to my folks through talking to him about them, and I'm learning more respect and compassion and everything for them now that I'm giving a little thought to how it would be without them.

Collin brought a soft blanket, and together we spread it out on a cement pad nestled in some trees. Collin said he thought the city would probably eventually build a little toolshed or something there, but for now it would give us a place to be comfortable and safe from the chiggers and no-see-ums.

It was so peaceful and lovely: birds singing, bees buzzing, water lapping, fish jumping, a little breeze blowing the branches that almost reached down to touch us. Us lying there eating potato chips and drinking Cokes, and Collin started rubbing my back. It felt good, warm, relaxing and belonging. I realized that I didn't get touched much by my mom anymore; she was so busy. But it was a different touch too. I felt happy little noises, almost like purring, splattering out of my mouth. The sounds came out without my even trying to make them. Collin laughed and rubbed my arms. It felt so, so, so good. When he got to my legs I felt a little bit uncomfortable, though. A strange little quivering shot through me, and I popped up suddenly. It embarrassed me, and I think it embarrassed him too . . . but again, it probably didn't. He probably didn't feel what I felt at all.

I wish I could talk to El or Dorie or Red. I want to talk to at least El, so much that it hurts, but I can't. I know that they would just try to convince me that Collin is too old for me and stuff . . . but nothing . . . nothing . . . *absolutely nothing* in the whole world can ever stop me from seeing him. I know I'm not supposed to date until I'm sixteen, but this isn't really dating. It's . . . I don't know what it is. I wish I did! I wish even more that I could talk with the kids about it, but they wouldn't understand my deepest deep feelings, and they *couldn't possibly* understand Collin! He's so mature. But maybe I'll try. I want to . . . I need to . . . I really do.

Saturday, April 21

10:01 A.M.

I'm crossing my fingers, I'm crossing my toes . . . and my eyes. I'm wishing and wanting you-know-who to call. *Please, please* call.

10:30 A.M.

Collin is psychic. We have a special, special bond between us. He felt that I was trying to contact him, and he *called* me! He really did! Isn't that almost scary? We can communicate mentally. I've heard of these things, but I've never experienced them before. We're both going to cut school Monday, and he's going to rent a little rowboat, and we're going to go up the river. I'm going to take a picnic breakfast and lunch in my book pack, and he's going to meet me at the bus stop at 8:45, just fifteen minutes after my school bus leaves. I wish it could be fifteen minutes before or an hour before or two or three . . . or *right now!* I can't wait. I know I'll never be able to sleep.

Sunday, April 22

1:45 A.M.

I was right. It's 1:45 A.M., and I can't sleep. I hope Collin isn't making a mistake in missing a day's school. I'm worried. I know he said he had a light class load tomorrow and that he can easily make up his work tomorrow night and stuff, but I really don't want him to get into any trouble or behind. College is serious. I'll have to encourage him.

It's 3:30, and I *still* can't sleep. I've relived every minute of every hour that I've known Collin. I wonder if maybe he'll change his mind . . . no, I won't even let myself think of that.

I'll think of the other afternoon in the park when it started raining. We were sitting in the Pavilion having Cokes, and he was being very formal and courteous like he always is when we're around someone. He's so shy! I wouldn't dare tell him, but sometimes he almost seems like he's my father. I'm sure it would hurt him if he knew that, because he's just trying to be a real Southern gentleman, so I don't say, I *won't* say, anything. I'll just live for the moments when we can be alone, and he can be his own true, sweet, loving, tender, understanding, compassionate, funny, fun self: Like, halfway through our Cokes he whispered seriously to me, "The sun shines brighter around you, the grass is greener, my appetite is healthier." He got a mischievous look in his eye. "So let's dash off and get a hot dog on the other side of the pond."

It was hard for us to walk seriously through the door and to the big tree beyond the turn in the path; then we laughingly loped off, hand in hand, through the warm, sticky rain to find a hot-dog stand in the park that was still open.

Many words like *life, fun* and *funny* have all taken on completely new and wonderful meanings since I met Collin.

4:10 A.M.

How could a Sunday ever be sooooo endless.

Monday, April 23

7:01 A.M.

It is finally Monday ... THE DAY.

8:49 P.M.

What a wonderful day. I am sure it is one of the most perfect days that the Creator ever created. I spread our breakfast out on *our* special place. Collin had to go back to the car for something, and as I watched him turn up the little jogging path coming back toward me, my heart leaped like a wild bird trapped in a too small cage. For the first time, I raced toward his outstretched arms and hugged him tightly—unembarrassingly. I had put *his* daisy in my hair. *"My* daisy. *My* Nancy," he whispered faintly. *We were family!*

A whole new and exciting dimension has been added to my life. It is beyond comprehension!

After breakfast we got into our little canoe and Collin soon paddled into the bayou area. We found a little island and landed. I felt like a combination of a Creole princess and an Indian maiden. After I'd stumbled into a little swampy puddle, Collin called me "Princess Mud on Nose and Toes." I called him "Great White Paddler." Together we explored our sovereignty and named it Nancol. I had more fun than I've ever had before. Collin wanted to do everything I wanted to do, explore when I wanted to explore, stop when I wanted to stop, go when I wanted to go, eat where I wanted to eat. I've never had a friend before who *wanted* to do *everything my way,* and said *that* made him happy!

Collin had brought his blow-up mattress, and just as he was getting ready to put it down, a cloud of gnats and mosquitoes swarmed around us in huge black clouds. It was like a nightmare movie as we tried to get at least part of our things together and run for the boat. After Collin had paddled down the river a bit, he stopped so we could get some of the pesky little critters out of our eyes and noses and hair. One had gotten in my ear and was buzzing around, making the noise of an airplane. Collin had to get it out with a bobby pin. Well, the gnats and mosquitoes kind of ruined our day, but *nothing* could ruin it really! Besides, we'd have had to leave in an hour or so anyway.

Collin, on the way home, sweetly said he'd call me in the afternoon right after I got off the bus, so we could talk before my mom got there.

I gave him a big grin, even though I felt like I had gnats in my teeth, and told him that we could talk as long as we wanted because Mom was going to be in the city getting final papers signed with a prospective buyer, and I was going to sleep over at El's. I told him I'd planned on going over there right after school, but I could take care of that. El lived just a few blocks away, and I'd ride (to her house) on my bike after we'd talked.

Collin grinned back at me and told me that would be "mag, in fact super mag." It made me glad that he'd picked up at least one thing from me. I'd picked up so much from him. Of course, mine were good things and his was just a dumb word. Oh well . . . so be it . . . or whatever.

10:10 A.M.—English

I've never had a dull, boring, humdrum schoolday pass so slowly in my life. I don't think one thing in one class registered. I can't wait to get home and talk to my bro—but in a way he's more than a brother, or is this how a really truly close, close family relationship feels? I wish I had someone to talk to who understands about these things, but I don't know who that would be. I hope he doesn't remember what a bawl baby I was and how I completely panicked when the black swarm of insects absorbed us. I *really* lost it! It's a good thing he's not a boyfriend or he would have dumped me verbally on the island or *physically* in the bayou, and I made such a sappy, dumb sap of myself, and I looked so gruesome with gnats in my eyebrows and my hair and stuff. How could he ever even want to talk to me again . . . ever?

2:13 P.M.—Math

I was so preoccupied and hyper during lunch that El and Dorie and Red were trying to hold me down in my chair in the cafeteria. Sometimes they seem *so childish,* without a care in the world or a thought in their heads. On the top of the blackboard, Mr. Nelson had the sign: ALGEBRA, THE REUNION OF BROKEN PARTS. 1. THE BRANCH OF MATHEMATICS THAT USES POSITIVE AND NEGATIVE NUMBERS, LETTERS, AND OTHER SYSTEMIZED SYMBOLS TO EXPRESS AND ANALYZE THE RELATIONSHIP BETWEEN CONCEPTS AND QUANTITY IN TERMS OF FORMULAS, EQUATIONS, ETC.: GENERALIZED MATHEMATICS.

Who cares? Who wants to tell the height of a telephone pole from its shadow? Who in their right mind would want to be in a dumb old math class if they could be out in the sun, having fun with someone like Collin? He's more beautiful than the picture of a young Greek god in our history books, or the statue of David in Florence, Italy. I saw that when we went there three years ago. It didn't seem like much then, but it does now, except that Collin is a little thinner.

I just looked up, and Mr. Nelson gave me a big smile. He thinks I'm working. If only he knew how far away my mind is from here. Well, really I am working in a way to get out at 3. I don't think I'll even go back to home room. Twenty-four minutes and I'm outta here. Nineteen long minutes left. I think I'll die.

4:32½ P.M.

Just as I raced in the house all hot and sweaty, the phone rang. Guess who? *Who else?* He said he'd called twice before I got in, but I couldn't have gotten here any faster if I'd been able to fly. It's like Christmas and all the birthday parties in the world combined, with the Fourth of July sparklers and fire-crackers thrown in.

Collin is going to come over and fix dinner for just the two of us! He says he's the world's fanciest, smanciest cook, and it will be a dinner we'll never forget, a special, special dinner that will be our very favorite till the end of time. And it will be! It truly will be, even if we have cow pies for dessert. Oh, why did I think that, it's childish and *not* funny. I'm just hysterical, crazy, happy hysterical, but hysterical or not, I better go in and clean up the breakfast dishes and throw my bed together and my clothes that are on the floor under the bed or something, or blessed Collin will walk in and walk right out again. Talk to you later, dear Self. 'Bye.

Wednesday, April 25

1:30 A.M.

Blackness, cold, jellied blackness has settled in over the world, and I don't know what to do . . . what to think, how to act . . . who to call. It started out so wonderfully . . . was that in another life? Another place? Another me? I'm so confused . . . so alone . . . I was going to say "so scared and hurting," but I'm really not *feeling anything*. It's weird! It's like I'm really *not me* anymore! Where have *I* gone? Who is this stranger who's writing? Will the real me, the happy, lighthearted, ditsy little-girl me, ever come back?

How did life go from total happiness and light to total darkness and whatever this horrible feeling that I'm feeling is? Let's start from the very beginning. As the song says, "A very good place to start." My grandma used to sing that to me when I was little and had a problem. PROBLEM? I didn't even know what a problem was then. Okay . . . be realistic, uncluttered . . . spit it out!

I'd slicked up the house and froo-frooed myself in my new chiffon gypsy skirt, and the sun was shining and the music of life was playing, and Collin came with a bag full of groceries, looking like the cover of *GQ* magazine, only better.

Maybe from then on, I brought this blackness on myself, and I can get rid of it. *Maybe* somehow I can make it light again, someday *somehow!!!*

Anyway, Collin fixed steak and mushrooms and salad and garlic bread, and I put out Mom's best dishes and goblets and candles. We laughed and fed each other, and he kissed each one of my fingers and told me something wonderful about myself with each kiss. It was brotherly ... but it wasn't too.

It was fun. Like playing house for real, with real music and real laughter and real wine cooler in Mom's beautiful, real champagne glasses.

I didn't tell Collin that I'd only tasted liquor once before. Last New Year's Eve Red and I sneaked some of her dad's Jack Daniel's and tried it, but it was hot and nasty, and we both just felt silly and dumb. She threw up, and I fell asleep on the floor and caught a bad cold.

But with me and Collin it's like, now that I'm looking back at it ... like a movie or something. I'm watching what happened, and it's not real. . . .

Collin was so sweet and so kind and so caring about what I thought and how I felt at first. *I want it to be that way again!* I want to feel wanted and needed and loved and important and that I'm number one in somebody's life ... in *his* life. I'll do whatever is necessary to bring it back to that. I will! I will!

It was soooooo beautiful. We danced, and we rubbed each other's back and feet, and he kept saying things to me that made me feel like a fairy princess and the most wonderful thing in the world. I've never felt so powerful and confident and priceless.

After a while, he lit a fire in our little fireplace and oops—I remembered I was supposed to spend the night with El.

Scared to death that her mom might drop by to pick me up before I could call her, I dialed the phone frantically. What would she think if she dropped in? And she might; she had a key for emergencies.

It seemed like the phone rang one hundred times before anyone answered, but she finally did.

I told her I had real bad cramps, and I wanted to sleep in my own bed.

At first she seemed unsure; then she made me promise to go put the night latches on both doors, and she waited on the phone for me to do it. It was funny, Collin and I giggling quietly as we tiptoed to each door and bolted it.

Finally, Mrs. Warner wished me good night and hung up, and Collin and I crumpled on the floor in fits of laughter.

We were on our second bottle of wine cooler, but it was more than that that made us so happily happy. It was just being together. He said I made him feel much, much, much more fulfilled and happy than he made me. I don't know how that could possibly be possible, but if he says so . . .

I made Collin promise that he would leave at the stroke of midnight. I knew our old grandfather clock wouldn't let him forget or try to cheat, because at twelve o'clock sharp it goes through a series of gongs and chimes that no one could ignore.

Collin put on Mom's Natalie Cole tape, and we danced for a while. He had turned out all the lights, and with just the glow from the fireplace and the shiny twinkling from the stars just a stone's throw away from our balcony, it was heaven.

Collin mixed a little bottle of something in our wine cooler, and it kind of ruined the taste, but at this point I couldn't say or even think anything negative. He had started becoming a little handsy, and I liked it . . . but I didn't like it too.

He pulled me down on the floor and explained to me about our relationship, how it had grown from a brother-sister type thing to a loving, respecting girl-boy thing. That made sense at that time, in that place and that condition. We drank a little more and listened to music and snuggled together, just loving and kissing. Dumb me, Collin even had to teach me how to kiss, but he was so gentle and patient and even fun and funny about it that I wasn't even embarrassed. He said in some movies people kiss like they're cannibals, and they're trying to eat each other.

We giggled, and I told him about the time El and I had watched an X-rated movie on cable when we were baby-sitting. It was gross and perverted and disgusting, but it was nice having someone mature like Collin to discuss it with.

It seemed like only seconds had passed when the clock started chiming midnight. I scrambled to my feet, tipsily walked toward the door to hold it open for him.

The next thing I knew, Collin had picked me up bodily and was carrying me into my mother's room. I struggled like crazy . . . I wanted to . . . but I didn't want to . . . Collin whispered I should . . . I cried I shouldn't. . . .

Collin dropped me down on my mother's soft flowered comforter, and I fought back with all my might. Red neon thoughts flashed through my mind . . . committing fornication on my own mother's bed . . . I was still a good little Catholic girl who had been taught that sexual impurity was not simply a venial sin easily pardoned, and to commit it on my own mother's bed . . . never . . . I wouldn't!

The whole scene keeps going over and over in my brain like a stuck record. My pleading, then screaming, "No, Collin, no. Please. Please, Collin . . . don't."

After a while, Collin pulled back and looked at me like I had hit him in the face with a crowbar or something. He seemed mortally wounded. "You mean you don't love me?"

I could feel his pain. I'd felt just like he looked when Catsup, my red kitten, had been squashed in the busy street and no one had stopped. I'd felt then that no one had ever loved me or would ever love me . . . or Catsup.

In spite of myself, I blubbered, "Yes . . . I guess I love you . . . but . . ." He started again, and I tried to squirm away, hitting and pushing. "Collin, I'm only fourteen, I'm only in junior high school . . . I shouldn't . . . I don't want to . . . it's . . . I think it's a mortal sin." Tears and snot were running down my face. It was awful, but he didn't seem to care. I tried every way I knew to get away. I even bit him . . . but he . . . raped me—NO, NO, *he didn't*. He wouldn't do that! Collin is not a *rapist*. I won't even think the word. He couldn't be that. He's kind and thoughtful and . . . but he really is a *rapist*. No, I brought it on myself. I must have made him think . . . no, I didn't. He really didn't have a right . . .

It was like he was somebody else. Not Collin, not sweet, thoughtful, kind Collin. He was a stranger who hurt me, hurt me a lot, all over, and he didn't even care.

I don't know him. Maybe I never did know the real him. But that's not so strange. I don't even know myself now.

Oh, how I wish I had talked to my friends. How I wish I had stayed over at El's. I couldn't have kept my secret from her all night. At some time I would have had to creep from my twin bed to hers and tell her every single detail about the last few days—about the concert, about Collin, abut my feelings.

I'm so, so, so confused . . . and hurt. My feelings are hurt almost more than my body, and it's pretty hurty. I could hardly walk to the bathroom. Oh chips, why does life have to be such a pile of chips anyway?

3 A.M.

It's 3 A.M., and I can't sleep. I don't think I'll ever be able to sleep again. I've cleaned up the house, gotten rid of every single thing that remains of . . . him. I even took the trash to the canister outside the building. I don't want it anywhere near me. Or any other reminder of . . . anything.

When it was over, he just got up and left. No good-bye. No "I'm sorry." No nothing.

If I'd just talked to my mom about Collin, maybe none of this would have happened. Maybe she'd have known how to handle things. How would I know? Sometimes I think I'm so smart-assed, and I try to pretend that I know everything, and there's no way I can be wrong, but chips, I've only lived fourteen years on this planet. I'm just a kid. Well, maybe I'm not a kid anymore. I guess *now* I'm a woman. Anyway, Mom probably wouldn't have known either.

I wonder if I should go to a priest. Mom and I aren't much into church, but maybe he could tell me what to do. I wonder if I could unload and reload on El . . . no, she'd just be angry and hurt that I hadn't talked to her sooner. Besides, how could she know anything about anything? She's as dumb and naive as me. But I did go to Catholic parochial school till the sixth grade. The nuns should have taught us something about something.

4:20 A.M.

I tried bed again, but it's no use. I had one moment of wanting to go get in Mom's bed and snuggle up to a pillow, pretending it was her. It's so peace-giving to crawl in with her when there are thunder and lightning storms and stuff, but I couldn't . . . I just couldn't! I wonder if I'll ever be able to sleep in her bed again, even go into her room. It's like now, for sure, all the boogeymen in the world will be in there.

5:10 A.M.

I'm so tired I can hardly keep my eyes open, but I still can't sleep. I wonder if it would be easier to go to school and suffer through the day or just stay here and do it. I guess staying here is better, because I know everyone at school could tell from my body language and stuff what had happened to me.

Guess I better call El's mom in an hour or so and tell her the big lie, *that I'm all right,* but that I won't be going to school today, another big lie, because I've still got the cramps. Uggg, I don't want to even think about any of my body parts, true or false. It's so animalistic.

5:59 A.M.

I've been pacing around the house. I can't sleep. I can't read. I can't watch TV. I can't think. It's like I'm another person. Like *you're* another person. Like you're my real self, and I'm just . . . just a bunch of meat and bones stumbling through a strange house filled with things that belong to strangers.

6:30 A.M.

Dear Self:

I've got to talk with someone. Maybe talking with you will do it. Who else can I talk to before the cocks crow, or whatever it is that changes night into morning.

I used to be such a positive, happy little kid, and now it's like I'm just an empty box of loneliness. Why didn't he say good-bye—or thanks—or I love you—or something?

Once I saw a real freak movie about some living-dead zombie people. That's how I feel, exactly how I feel, ugly, unworthy, unlovely. I want to die.

7:13 A.M.

I took another shower, and I put on another clean pair of pajamas, but I still feel dirty. I tried to look up "mortal sin" in both the dictionary and the encyclopedia, but they don't tell about it. I wonder if Catholics are the only ones who have to pay the price for mortal sins. The dictionary says under *mortal*, "Number six: causing death of the *soul;* said of sin; distinguished from venial." Under *venial,* the dictionary says, "That which may be forgiven; pardonable; as a venial sin; in theology, opposed to mortal."

Oh, dear Self. I remember Sister Theresa telling us the difference between mortal sin and venial. I wish I had listened more and remembered more. If the dictionary says under *mortal*, "Causing *death of the soul,"* is that what's happened to me? I'm only fourteen years old; how could my soul possibly be dead?

But maybe it can! The littlest innocentest baby can have something horrible happen to it, I don't remember what, if it isn't baptized. Dear Self, can't you remember either? Please try. Please, please try.

7:41 A.M.

I called El's mom and asked her to have El take an excuse to school for me. I lied last night about being sick, but I'm *not* lying this morning.

8:02 A.M.

I feel soooo much better. I looked up the St. Peter's Parish number in the phone book. Sister Martha answered, and I just blurted out that I'd been raped, but maybe I really hadn't—and I had to know if it was a mortal sin and my soul was dead. Then I blubbered, and I didn't make a lot of sense. She tried to calm me and tell me that *God would forgive me* and I *hadn't* lost my soul and I *wasn't* going to hell, and all like that!

She told me to come and see the priest, but I said I didn't have a ride and I didn't know how to get there. She was so sweet and kind. She told me not to worry about anything and that everything would be all right, just to put all my trust in God and Jesus.

Self, you can't believe how much better I feel. How relieved. It's bad enough to have to deal with the here and now without having to deal with the hereafter, especially "death of the soul" and stuff like that, that I can't even understand.

4 P.M.

I can't believe that I've slept the entire day away. I guess I'd still be asleep if Mom hadn't come in and awakened me ... woke me? Anyway, I was so glad to see her I couldn't believe it. I hugged her and kissed her, and she cozily hugged me on the couch while she told me all about her trip and the wonderful deal she had put through. I put my head down on her lap, and she brushed my hair like I love for her to do. "One, two, three, four, five, I'm so glad that you're alive. Six, seven, eight, nine. My little girl is doing fine. Eleven, twelve and then, we get to start all over again."

The hurt was beginning to heal, and I had thought it never would.

8:06 P.M.

Mom and I ordered pizza and ate out on the terrace in our pajamas. She was exhausted from her trip. We cleaned up the kitchen together, and it was fun. Then I helped her unpack her briefcase and papers in her little office, but I couldn't go into her bedroom. I stopped at the door and felt like I was going to throw up. I wonder if I'll ever be able to go in there again.

After Mom had gone in, I stood outside her door trembling, wondering if she'd be able to feel anything different, anything evil. I guess she didn't, because in a little while I heard her climbing into bed. I wanted so much to go climb in with her, but I couldn't do that ... not now ... not yet. I hope someday ... I really do hope someday.

11:30 P.M.

I watched a couple of TV shows, but they were really dumb. It's funny about life. I used to want so much to be grown up. I resented it every time Mom did her mothering thing. I hated it when she tried to tell me, show me or example me, and I told her so, sometimes in a not too kind or considerate way.

Now I *want* to be treated like a little kid. I *want* to be protected and coddled and told and asked and all the things I used to think I didn't want! I used to pull away from Mom's hugs, be embarrassed about her efforts to give pats and squeezes; now I *want* them desperately, *need* them lifesavingly!

When did I start stupidly thinking I was so high-and-mighty and know-it-all, that I could be on my own, do it myself? Think that I didn't need her, or anybody else, to give me advice or guidance? Oh, what a dumb, dumb idiot I've been and unappreciative and irresponsible and conceited! How could Mom ever love me or want me? Maybe she doesn't . . . maybe nobody does. But how could they ever love me or want me . . . I don't even love or want myself.

Friday, April 27

11:10 A.M.

Dear Self:

It's been three long, long, long, dull, dull, dull, boring, boring, boring days since . . . you know. I haven't been out of the apartment. Mom thinks I've got the stomach flu. I'm so bored and uptight I'm about ready to go back to school. I would, but I can't face anybody yet. Not Red, or Dorie or El or anybody! My life has changed. It's forever changed. I'm, for some crazy reason, not really *me* anymore. It's kind of nightmare movie-ish. Will I always feel this lonely and empty? It's funny how one day the sun is shining and the world is filled with birds singing and bells ringing, and then ... blam ... you're sucked down into some deep never-never land of darkness and pain, where not even a shadow of light can get through.

1:30 P.M.

I've been sitting by the phone waiting for two hours ... waiting for what? I hate to even admit it, but I'm waiting for Collin to call. I know he must be feeling as awful as I do. I go look by the front door every minute. I have this feeling that he's going to come and leave another little brown-paper-wrapped box with one single white daisy in it and a heartbroken note. I know he just let his emotions get away with him ... his animalistic, powerful emotions that he couldn't control. *He'll call!* We'll talk about everything, and he'll cry and I'll cry and we'll figure out what to do. So he did a dumb, stupid, out-of-control thing. . . .

I know he's heartbroken! He's bright, and his life is in such order, but he's shy too, and I can just imagine how humiliated he is. Poor Collin. He must be as mixed up as I am, and hurting. He must be terribly hurting ... and confused ... and ashamed. That's it! He's just trying to get his act together like I am. Oh, I feel so much better knowing that!

2:26 P.M.

I can't stand it any longer. Collin has suffered
enough. I'm sure he's in as bad shape as I am. He
can't eat, he can't study . . . and he's got to study!
He's worked so hard getting scholarships and everything, he can't waste them now because . . . well, because of something that was probably mostly my
fault. I . . . well, I turned him on . . . and then . . . I'm
such a dork.

When we were sitting in the park that very first
time, when he told me he didn't want to tell me but
that he had to share with someone . . . oh, how sweet
that was to have him tell me about all his goals for the
future and stuff. How he wanted to be a doctor . . . and
on and on. The very best part of what he said was that
from the very first moment he saw me leaning lostly
against the concert wall, he wanted to protect me, have
me part of his lifelong plans from that moment on.
Dear Collin. We need to talk. We can get this whole
mess straightened out. I know we can! Maybe we can
just be friends, dear, precious, wonderful, bosom-buddy
friends for a couple of years . . . well, at least till I'm
in high school or something. Anyway, I know we can
put it back together! I just have this wonderful, positive, white-light feeling that we can. That we must!

3:02 P.M.

I think I'm going to call Collin. Do I dare? I not
only dare, I've got to! I can! I will! I wish he had a
phone in his hall. But I don't even know which hall
he's in. If I did I could go by and leave a note or
something.

What a selfish, self-centered, empty-box person
I've been. We just talked about me, always me, what

I liked, how I felt, about my mom, my dad—me, me, me, marshmallow-headed me. But that's what he said he wanted . . . to know every little last-minute detail of my life so that he could feel part of the wonder of it. I dare you, Self. Okay. One, two, three, dial—

4:59 P.M.

The lights have all gone off again. I can't believe it! I've made some mistake somewhere. I'm sure Collin said ——————— University. Maybe not, but what else could it have been? We've only got one university here. I'm sooooo confused. I just called the university, and they said they had no Collin Eagle at all registered there. I had the lady check three times. They have never heard of him. He is not living in campus housing. He is not in student government. He is not on the Dean's List. I can't understand it. How did I mess up so badly? Where else could he be? Could it be junior college? No. No, he definitely said ———————. Ohiihhh, I think I'm going to die. I've lost my mind. I've, like, gone completely crazy over this thing. I can't think straight. If Collin is not at the university, where is he? Did he just drop out and leave after . . . no, they said he never had been registered there. Then . . . I wish Mom were here. I need to talk to her. I want to talk to her as much now as I used to not want to talk to her. Oh, Mom . . . please hurry, please, please hurry home. I need you.

After I'd thrown up a couple of times, I finally called Mom. I couldn't believe how fast she got home. What a lucky, lucky person I am to have her to lean on, to love me, to understand and not condemn and scream and rant and rave and tear her hair—and mine. She just hugged me and rocked me and cried with me as I poured out the whole strange, weird, awful mess, and she just kept saying over and over that it wasn't my fault, that I shouldn't blame myself, that I'll be all right, that she would protect me and help me heal.

She tried to take all the blame on herself because she'd been gone so much and such, but I can't let her do that. If a kid wants to do some crazy thing, she'll find a way. Like me—cutting school and stuff.

Saturday, April 28

2:29 A.M.

Dear Self:
I can't sleep anymore, and I didn't want to thrash around in the bed and wake Mom, so I'm talking with you.

Mom and I talked for hours, then we took our baths, and she tucked me into her bed like she used to when I was very, very little. I felt so small and protected that all the other stuff didn't seem real. She sang to me about "the mama kitty says to her baby, Meoooow means I love you, close your eyes, go to sleep." And by the time she'd gone through the dog and the sheep and the mouse and the bee, I think I dropped into little-kid lala land. It was so comforting and belonging. I wish I could have stayed there forever, but, of course, I couldn't! And I can't! So here I am. In the middle of the night wide awake and wondering who the heck I am . . . and where the heck I'm going . . . and will it ever get morning.

7:30 A.M.

Mom woke up at seven, right after I'd gone to sleep. She shook me, called me her "precious little sleepyhead" and said during the night she made plans for us to leave the old world behind and whip out into the wild blue yonder on a wacky and whimsical adventure.

She's given me exactly one half hour to dress and pack some shorts and swimsuits and sweats, so I guess I'd better get started. It sounds fun. Mom can be lots of fun when she tries . . . no, when I let her.

9 P.M.

I don't think even Mom realized what a wacky and whimsical adventure we were starting out on. First she called El's mom and asked her to have me excused from school for a few days. Then we went by her office, and she told them she was leaving for a few days, and there was no way she could be reached because even she didn't know where she was going.

Three hours later we arrive at Azule Beach. It was really funny. We went from one hotel and motel to another with no luck. Finally, just as we were beginning to think we were going to have to sleep in the car, we found a little old ramshackle, run-down cottage on the beach that had a ROOM FOR RENT sign in the window. It looked spooky, almost like the witch's cottage in *Hansel and Gretel,* but it was on a wild, windswept, sand-dunish side, and we decided it would be fun.

After Mom and I had been out racing with the waves and tide for a couple of hours, we picked up a couple of hamburgers and went back to our fairy-tale-like, humble little abode. I went into the bathroom to put some vaseline on my lips and a little mouse peeked out at me as I opened the rickety old medicine chest. He was as startled by me as I was by him, and for a second we just stared at each other, first with fear, then wonder, then delight. At least for me it was delight. He might have then run off into a hole somewhere and had a heart attack, but I don't think so. I'm going to leave hamburger crumbs out for him tonight and maybe I can make him my friend. I liked him. I'd never seen a real live mouse up nose-to-nose close before ... he's sweet and I've named him *MICKEY* ... original, huh?

Sunday, April 29

7:32 A.M.

Mom's a teensy-weensy bit upset; she's trying not to show it, but it seems Mickey brought a few of his friends into our bathroom last night to have a party with my leftover hamburger. They cleaned up the hamburger; then they all left their little calling cards on the floor. Mom wasn't amused when she stepped on them in her bare feet. I was! I fell on the floor laughing, which is funny in itself, because I honestly hadn't thought I would ever laugh again.

I remember a couple of days ago I tried. Could that have been a couple of days? It seems like a couple of years. Anyways, I remember I stood in front of the mirror and tried to smile and only a crooked grimace came out. It was a very sad excuse of a smile, and try as I would, I couldn't make it any better. Now, I'll forever smile when I think of Mom almost slipping on the gooey wet little mouse droppings.

At first she wanted outta here; then she started seeing the fun and funny side of it, and we both rolled on the bed laughing so hard we were crying. When she got up, though, she made me promise we'd in the future give Mickey and his friends their party packs on the little porch outside our door to the beach. At first I said no, I was going to feed them in her twin bed. Then I relented, nice, empathetic person that I am . . . ummm. I wonder what would happen if I did put crumbs up to her bed and then in it . . . I couldn't do that . . . or could I? Not if I wanted to stay at the beach, I couldn't.

Tuesday, May 1

6 A.M.

I can't believe four days have passed so quickly. The first day here we saw some girls making seaweed baskets. They showed us how and we've made little treasure presents to take home. On some we've entwined shells and starfish and exotic things, and they're beautiful, even if they do stink. The girls said that would go away.

We get up as the blackness of night begins to turn into the grayness of day and search all the little tide pools for jewels of the sea. We really do feel like adventurers in a new world. I hardly ever think of Collin . . . well, at least not all the time like I did at home.

I'm so confused about him . . . about us. Has he tried to call me a million times since I've been gone? Or . . . did he just use me? Go away, negative, ugly thoughts, we don't have time or room for you here. Our cottage is too small and too magic.

We've got our chest and the bathroom-sink counter

covered with baskets. Mom's only fear is that Mickey
and his friends will feel obligated to fill them with
their presents.

11:39 A.M.

Oh, I don't want to leave. I want to stay here forever. With just Mom and me and the sand and the sun
and the sea gulls—and Mickey and his crew. I'm going to miss them! I really am going to miss them! We
don't often see them, but we always know they've
been here. How? Calling cards, remember? I think
I'll ask Mom to get me a pet when we get back. A
mouse? A gerbil? A cat . . . a dog . . . a horse . . . an
elephant? Maybe I should start asking for an elephant
so she will be relieved to finally have me accept a
kitten or a gerbil. Smart thinking, yes? No?

10:40 P.M.

We're home and home is HOME again! I'm so relieved. Something inside of me was afraid that it
would always be filled with . . . you-know-who . . .
doing you-know-what. But he doesn't exist anymore.
It was all a black, scary, fuzzy nightmare, and eventually it will go away, like the nightmares I had when
I was little did . . . I pray it will.

Wednesday, May 2

7:01 P.M.

El and Red and Dorie were all soooooo glad to see
me. We went to the mall after school and looked at
all the things we wanted to buy and couldn't. I finally
bought, after three hours, one tiny little tank top to

wear the next time Mom and I go to the beach. I hope we go to the very same beach and the very same cottage.

9:14 P.M.

I was working on a problem, and suddenly a picture of Mom and me trying to do my homework in our crazy little beach house popped into my head. Mom was *really* trying, probably trying even harder than I was, but neither one of us could get it. I got disgusted and said it was like a foreign language. Mom said it was even worse than that. It was like asking a baby to read, and I said it was like trying to make gold out of straw like in *Rumpelstiltskin,* and Mom said it was like trying to make a silk purse out of a sow's ear. We both gave up at that and laughed, because neither one of us knew what it meant, although we'd both heard Grandma Mamie say it a million times.

I'll always remember that day. It was a nice memory. Once when Dad and Mom and I had been backpacking in the Grand Canyon, and I was so scrawny that sometimes they had to backpack me, Dad had looked up at the golden peaks piercing up through the golden sky and said, *"We are making memories."* I wonder if Mom ever thinks of those times like I do.

Saturday, May 5

8:10 A.M.

Dear Self:

As you know, I started taking flute lessons in February and I've progressed so fast that Mr. Miller let me play with the band at State today. It was really exciting. All the bands from around the area in runoffs. We only came in fifth, but it was fun. I met lots of kids from this area, and Dorie and I checked out everything there was to check out. We felt a little lonely without El and Red, but neither one of them is into the band bit. But you know all this dribble, don't you?

I can't believe it—five more days and I'll be fifteen. Wow! Then just one more year and I'll be able to drive. Me ... driving ... non-dependent ... free! Being able to go where I want to go, when I want to go—that is, if and when Mom lets me take her car. Pop ... there goes another hot-air bubble.

Oh well, I will still be fifteen and in the last year of junior high school next year when school starts.

Sunday, May 6

Nothing.

Monday, May 7

Nothing. My life is one nothing after another nothing.

Tuesday, May 8

I'm really hurt. I asked Mom if we could do something special for my birthday, and she said she'd see.

I asked the gaggle (Mom always calls me and El and Red and Dorie the "gaggle of girls," sometimes the "goofy, giggling gaggle of girls") if they wanted to do something on the tenth, and none of them seemed interested. Chips, what's happened to us? We used to be a foursome of Siamese twins, kind of.

Wednesday, May 9

Another boring day of school. Not one person even mentioned my birthday. I guess maybe we're growing up, and birthdays aren't important anymore; at least mine doesn't seem to be.

Thursday, May 10

1:15 A.M.

What oz friends I have. I didn't think Mom or any of the gaggle could ever keep a secret two minutes, but they did this time! Did they ever! I had noooooo clue.

Before school, Mom asked if I'd like to go to a nice place for dinner, just the two of us. It didn't sound like much of a celebration, but it was better than nothing. She even offered to take me to the mall after school and buy me a new outfit, which, of course, was an offer I couldn't refuse. . . . I bought this really mag white pantsuit and a pair of maggy mag shoes. I couldn't tell Mom, but I felt they were too magnif just to go out to dinner with her.

We had an early dinner because Mom said she had an eight o'clock meeting tomorrow morning, and she had to prepare for it. And besides, she felt like she was coming down with a cold.

On our way home Mom said she just remembered that El had called and said she had an assignment that Miss Collier, our science teacher, had forgotten to give to me when we got home from the beach.

I didn't think it could be very important, but Mom said she thought it might be.

I didn't want to go into El's house. I was half mad at her because she hadn't wanted to do anything with me. The house was dark, and for a minute I was jealous. She'd probably gone out with some other kids when she should have been out with me, if she was any kind of a friend at all, which obviously she wasn't.

There weren't any cars around and no lights, and I almost didn't ring the bell. When I did, El answered the door and said dully, "Yeah, I've got something for you in here on the desk."

Sh hadn't even said hello or anything, and I was really beginning to think black-and-red explosive thoughts when suddenly all the lights turned on, and the roof almost disintegrated as everybody yelled, "HAPPY BIRTHDAY, NANCY."

I was so delighted and surprised, I almost wet my pants. Then El and I were hugging, and Red and Dorie and all the others were trying to hug me too. It was wild. Wild and magnif.

The first game we played was Who's Going Where, and Lew and I were teamed up. There were posters for mountain, stream, ocean, cliff, gorge and stuff, and in the house and all around the yard. Half the things I couldn't do, and Lew finally picked me up and carried me over the line. We won! But we never would have if he hadn't carried me.

Next Brian tried to carry Trish, and they both fell down! It was hilarious. I would have died if I had fallen down in my new white suit—that is, I would have died if Mom hadn't killed me first!

Later some of the kids played volleyball and some danced. Lew and I played table tennis. That made me happy because it's one of the things I do pretty well. He had to really concentrate to keep me from beating him. Thank goodness for the Ping-Pong table in the rec room of our apartment house.

I had such a wonderful, *wonderful* time! Lew asked me if I wanted to call my mom and tell her his older brother Mike would take me home. Did I? Did I ever!

Sitting in the front seat between Lew and his brother was heavenly! I thought I was going to float right off the planet. Lew walked me to the door and softly said, "I hope you had a nice birthday party, Nancy, because I really did."

I wanted to jump up and down and yell, "Yes, I did. I did! I did! I've never had such a mag party in my whole life." But, of course, I didn't; that *would not* have been FIFTEENISH!

Sunday, May 13—Mother's Day

What a lovely, sacred day. I've got the best mother in the world. After Mass, just the two of us went on a picnic and daylong hike. I'm soooo glad Mom is *my* mom.

Friday, May 18

Lew has lunch with me and El and Dorie and Red every day, and we all go home together on the same bus.

Today I was really embarrassed when Dorie said she thought we should make him one of the gaggle. He didn't seem to mind; in fact, he said superiorly that he thought that was an inspired suggestion. He told us a gaggle meant a "flock of geese or chattering company" and that he could buy that, if we'd let him be the token gander. We all agreed like we'd known all along what a gaggle meant, which I'm sure we didn't. I didn't even know what a gander was till I got home and looked it up in the dictionary. It's a male goose.

Saturday, May 19

12:15 P.M.

Tonight a bunch of us went to the show, except Lew and I didn't go to the show. We just walked around town and talked and stopped at Big Jack's and had a hamburger. He had onions, so I had onions too, even though I don't like them and wouldn't have touched one if I'd been with the gaggle.

Lew's been a part of my life from as far back as I can remember. We used to live just around the corner from him before Mom and Dad divorced me. I mean divorced each other. Lew's folks are divorced now too.

We had a little corner booth way in the back, and they weren't busy, so we just sat and talked for almost the whole movie time. It passed so quickly, but we had a lot to talk about. I'd forgotten that Lew taught me to ride my first tricycle, but I remembered his teaching me to ride my two-wheeler and telling me over and over that I could do it, after I'd fallen off and skinned my knee and my elbow a hundred times.

I remember really clearly sitting on my porch and watching him ride like the wind in and out of the trees and over curbs and doing wheelies and all sorts of other fancy stuff as we grew older. I really thought he was the greatest. I remember when we were in first grade we had said we were going to get married, but I didn't mention that until he did. We laughed and recalled how his big brother, who now chauffeured us, had to babysit us, and how much he had hated it. He'd have to take us to the park and watch us sometimes, while his buddies played ball. He called us brats and pigs and bugs ... sometimes even things we didn't dare tattle to his mother, but we didn't care; we just dug in the sand or went down the slides, feet-first, headfirst or tandem.

It was funny how Lew always took care of me then like he's beginning to take care of me now. He pushed me to put a paper in a school Literature project ... and I did ... and just like he said I would, I won honorable mention. He's so comfortable, and my life has become almost normal again.

Sunday, May 20

5:06 P.M.

Last night I told you my life was normal. Today it's the abnormalest it's ever been! Guess who I saw walking beside the river with Margie Muller? You're right! *Collin.* I wanted to run after him and scratch his eyes out. I wished I was an Arnold Schwarzenegger-type terminator so that I could squash his brains into the gravel walk and then squash the rest of him right into his empty head. With my next thought I wanted to grab Margie up in my arms and fly her away. Margie is two years younger than I am and only in *seventh* grade, just *one year* out of grade school ... she's a baby. Surely Collin wouldn't ... but something deep, deep inside tells me he would.

I hope and pray dear little thirteen-year-old Margie won't be as dumb and gullible as I was ... or is it already too late?

I wonder if I should call Margie's mother and tell

her about Collin, or should I call Margie? Would she believe me if I did, or would she just think I was crazy and jealous? Probably! If someone had called me (how stupid could I have been), I honestly don't think I would have believed one unkind thing about ... I can't even write his name. If I did, it would make me want to puke on the paper. Or on you! And you don't deserve that, dear Self. Now I'm writing like I am crazy! Maybe I am. I surely must have been in the past.

It made me literally sick to my stomach to see pukey blank walking along with Margie, appearing normal and deep-South friendly, at least on the outside, but ... maybe I was wrong. Maybe just *I* brought out the worst in him ... or asked for it ... or something. . . . Weird? . . . possibly? . . . probably!

Owww, I am so sick. I haven't had an attack like this in years. I better go to bed before I pass out. I'll do something about Margie in the morning.

Tuesday, May 22

3:01 P.M.

Two days have passed since I saw Margie and =*+*. Mom came home just in time to get me to the clinic. I had had an asthma attack that had almost closed my throat. She's being so sweet and so comforting, and she wouldn't let me talk if I could. What would I say anyway? It's all so strange and garbled in my heavily medicated brain. I can hardly read my own writing. I guess I better go back to my sleepytime escape hole. It's bright and soft and hidden in there, and no one can get in, and I can't get out.

When I get well I'm going to make it illegal to have nights.

Day? I dunno.

The last few days and nights my pillow has been wet with tears. Tears for Margie. Tears for me. I've had daymares and nightmares and feelings of guilt, guilt, guilt, guilt. The panic and the feelings of filthiness won't end. I'm guilty for Margie; I'm guilty for me too! And I CAN'T BEAR SUCH GUILT! I'm too small. I'm too weak. I'm too young.

I'm totally unworthy of the friendship of nice people like Red and El and Dorie, and especially Lew. Their parents wouldn't want me to go with them. I know that! If I were a parent, I wouldn't want *me* to go with *me*.

Saturday, May 26

My body's all right, but I can't seem to get my brain in gear. I can't get the pollution out of my mind. It's numbing me! Poisoning me! Crippling me! I don't want to think about *it*, but it keeps swirling around and around inside me like mud in a mixer. I really am losing touch with reality. I won't answer the phone and talk to anyone, and I won't see anyone, *ANYONE!* I can't have them see and hear how I've broken down physically and mentally.

I've heard of nervous breakdowns. I wonder if that is what this is. I can't face life anymore! I don't want to! I just want to sink away and become part of the black nothingness between the planets and the galaxies. I want my atoms to circle around through the eons as non-living things, no joys, no sorrows, no strains, no pain, no nothing, me nothing!

Sunday, May 27

A MIRACLE. I was lying in the living room looking aimlessly out the terrace sliding-glass door, in my obsession black funk, when I heard something hit against the glass. Startled and curious, I darted over and opened the door. A totally helpless, tiny little bright yellow-and-orange bird lay crumpled on the floor. It fluttered its fragile wings the tiniest little bit, then lay silent. I picked it up and cradled it in the palm of my hand. The precious little creature was softer than I knew soft could be and I begged it, pleaded with it, to breathe. I rubbed my finger over its little chest the way we were taught in CPR to do with a baby, but it was sooooooo small. I tried to give it mouth-to-mouth. Finally I just gently squeezed its little chest and prayed. "Don't die, little friend. Please, God, please don't let it die." I leaned over and kissed its soft little head. "Live for me. Please . . . I need you to. I really, truly, honestly do need you to." At that very moment the baby bird opened his tiny bright eyes and looked right into mine like he knew what I was saying. He didn't move, but I could feel his heart pounding in his miniature body. He lay so soft and still that I knew he needed me as much as I needed him.

Mom had come up behind me, and when she saw my new little buddy was moving, she whispered that she'd run down to the storeroom and get the cage in the corner that no one was using.

7 A.M.

Glory hallelujah. It's like we have a new baby in the house. Mom called her secretary and told her she'd be coming in late, and she said she'd give me an excuse so I could be late for school, and she'd drop me there.

We've been so busy trying to make-shift a little nest and stuff and a water bowl till the pet store opens that it's like Christmas or something.

I'm sitting here watching baby in his new home, and he seems perfectly happy and content. I expected him to be flapping against the sides trying to get out. He's so precious! He is a *miracle* to me!

Something within me wants me to slip back and wallow in the garbage of my encounter with Collin . . . but I won't let it! I shouldn't!

Snap out of it, you retarded girl-person. Where is your mind? Where is your heart? Where are your eyes? Where are your ears? You've been blocking out everything good in life and concentrating only on the ugly and the bad. That's sad. It's bogus mogus, and you nogus it. If this little fragile bird creature can get its life together after its smashup, surely you can too.

7:26 P.M.

Mom and I named our little gift from heaven Imperical.

No one but us will ever know what that really stands for. It's so special to share a wonderful secret with Mom. *Our little Imperical miracle!* Mom says *imperical* means: Magistic! August! Magnificent!

Isn't it spooky that Imperical means my favorite special words, *mag* and *magnif?*

Tuesday, May 29

Time truly goes quickly when you're having fun! I know that's an old, dumb saying, but it's true.

Gotta go. One of the gaggle is on the phone, Mom says.

Wednesday, May 30

3:55 P.M.

I feel so heavyhearted. I saw Margie today at school. It's pretty clear from her heavy steps and sagging posture that Collin has done her and dumped her too. I want to get everyone I know and go find him and emasculate him ... but no matter how guilty I feel about what happened to me and Margie, I've made a sacred oath to get out of the past and into my foreverish long future.

10:30 P.M.

I hope it doesn't take Margie as long to get over her garbage dump as it did me. I wonder if it would help if I talked to her. Maybe I will.

Wednesday, June 6

School's out. Time for fun and games!

Thursday, June 7

Red's parents took the gaggle up to her uncle Bill's cabin on the lake to celebrate. Did I say cabin? Five bedrooms and a living room that looks out over the lake. The house is as big as a football field. Well, maybe not *that* big, but fab and mag, and I've never had such fun.

Red's dad brought Lew up to help with the boats and do a little "fixing up around the place" while we girls just gaggle.

It's unbelievably beautiful here with the tall piney forest in the background and the luscious lake in front. I think if I could live anyplace in the world I wanted to, it would be some place like this. Maybe I'd retire and write or paint. Yes, I'd paint like my mom's aunt Thelma. She's so gifted she can see something once and paint it months later in the tiniest detail.

One summer, we spent a week with her up at her ranch in Idaho. She taught me wondrous things, like seeing little miniature flowers that I hadn't even known were hiding down in the weeds. Flowers so bitsy and fragile and perfect that it almost made me feel like I was living in *Gulliver's Travels,* with me the giant and them the normal size. Aunt Thelma had me take a picture of each flower or thing in my mind so that later I could describe them to her in the smallest detail. She also taught me to draw from my mental pictures as well as from *real* life, and it was an *unreal* experience! I hope to get to go back to Aunt Thelma's again soon.

The kids are swimming and boating and playing volleyball on the beach and hiking and all that wild stuff, but I'm enjoying just lying here in the sun with Rover and Rockey, the two big dogs that live here. They love me and lick me and try to get me to come lie in the shade with them. They don't realize that I need the heat because I don't have a beautiful gray fur coat like them.

Sunday, June 10

5:30 A.M.

Last night after dinner, Lew and I went for a long walk. We sat on a big rock looking out over the lake, watching the sun going down, and talked about all our dreams and our futures. Lew is so mature for his age and so wise. I guess that's maybe because his mom and dad both teach at the university, and his two brothers are older. Kyle is in college, and Mike, our old-time baby-sitter, is in his last year of high school. I think they talk about mostly adult things at their house.

Anyway, it was fun to think about what we'd be and where we'd be: after high school, after college, after marriage. Lew knows already that he wants to be a microbiologist. His uncle is one, and he's worked with him in the laboratory since he was a little kid. Germs and viruses and bacteria excite him. It's almost like they are people, instead of bugs.

I don't know what I want to be, but he's convinced me I better start thinking about it now, so I'll be assured of a career instead of just a job. Frankly, Self, I didn't know the difference until he explained that most jobs don't have much future growth for "one." He sometimes says "one" instead of "you." It sounds okay for him to do it but weird for me. Anyway, careers take more self-motivation and drive, but "one" can usually get higher and progress faster. Did you notice I said ONE, but only to you, only to you! . . . well, maybe to him . . . almost assuredly "one" with his family, if I can remember.

As I think about it, I've decided to go into the medical field too. I'm just not sure if I want to be a nurse or a doctor or do some kind of lab work. I think maybe becoming a doctor would take too long, because I really want to be a mother, but wouldn't being a pediatrician and then a mother be the greatest?

Lew and I both want to be parents. He wants to have three or four kids. He says it's good for there to be lots of kids in a family for a support group.

Lew told me about his parents' divorce and how much his brothers helped him through it. I cried instead and wished I had had something like that when my dad divorced us.

I was really surprised that Lew's parents had split. They always seemed so ideal to me. His aunt Mary Mack worked as their housekeeper and substitute mother, while Mr. and Mrs. or Dr. and Dr. Fullmark went off together to the university, sometimes in two cars, sometimes in one.

Lew said his mom's MS had gotten really bad after we moved, and his dad hadn't been able to handle it. I didn't even know she had MS, but after Lew mentioned it, I remembered she often walked with a little limp and held one hand funny sometimes.

My mom left Dad after he met Shelly. Mom never did talk about it, and Dad didn't stay with Shelly long . . . but who knows about adults and the stupid, crazy, thoughtless, hurtful things they sometimes do.

Lew and I talked about how guilty we felt after the breakups. Lew said he used to sit for hours wondering if he had been more polite, more grown up, more thoughtful and helpful and less quarrelsome and whiny with his brothers, if that would have helped. I said I'd always wondered if I had cleaned my room and taken better care of Catsup so they wouldn't have

53

had to do it, and not have been so rude and stuff, if that would have helped my parents stay together. We decided probably not. Anyways, we both know *we're* never, never, never going to get divorced once we're married! Parents don't seem to realize that when they divorced each other they divorce their kids too.

I just looked up *divorce* in the dictionary. It says, "Disunion, complete separation; to turn or go different ways; dissolution; disunite; to rid oneself." No wonder us kids feel so bad when we're divorced from one or both of our parents. "To rid oneself." Are we divorced from one or both of them if they are divorced from each other? I guess it doesn't matter, because we couldn't be any more hurt or confused, no matter what it was.

3:10 P.M.

Uncle Bill (everybody calls Red's uncle "Uncle" now) had a church service right in his home. I didn't know you, I mean "one," could do that. It was really beautiful, sacred and reverent. Red played the music on the piano, and Uncle Bill had Xeroxed the words for all of us. They were almost like prayers to music that we all sang together, from the deepest part of our hearts. It made me feel good to know that we all believe in God. I'd never put that belief into exact thoughts before, but I know it's true now.

For a sermon, Uncle Bill took a bottle of water and poured a little black ink or something into it. As he poured drop by drop, the water got dirtier and dirtier. Finally he said that was like sinning; every time we lied or cheated or stole or did anything unethical or unkind, a little more blackness came into our lives. Then he brought out a vial of bleach and said putting repentance into our lives was much like the bleach. It would help us to be white and clean and pure inside again. We then all discussed that concept and decided that we each needed to carry a little bottle of repentance around with us all the time, because *we needed it often!* Especially *me!*

We decided for the rest of the day when we spilled on someone or did something else dumb or rude or careless or mean, instead of saying, "I'm sorry," we'd say, "I repent of that action. Will you forgive me?" It was hard for El to do when Red slammed her finger in the boathouse door . . . but she finally did. That put a whole new meaning upon repentance and forgiveness. Now it makes sense. And I've felt GOOD, a DIFFERENT, BETTER KIND OF GOOD AND HAPPY ALL DAY.

We closed the service with the song "Happy Hearts Make Happy Homes," and I thought how wonderful it would be if we all had happy homes like Red's uncle Bill and aunt Lorna. They have pictures of their grown kids and grandkids all over the house, and they've been married for *fifty-three years to each other!* Can you imagine that kind of Happy Hearts Make Happy Homes stuff?

7:26 P.M.

When Lew and I went to sit on the boathouse steps, a full moon was hanging out over the lake. Its reflection was almost as bright as the moon itself, and Lew stood on his head just to make sure he could tell the difference. He could, barely.

He wanted to take a run on the beach with the dogs, who were bugging us to do that, bringing sticks to us to throw and all that stuff, but I didn't want to.

I just wanted to sit and be part of the moonlight and the fragrances and the strange snuggling sounds that were wafting down from a bird's nest. We had *wafting* as a spelling word once, and this is the first time in my life I've had a chance to use it. I thought then it was a dumb word, but it's a beautiful word, soft and musical. Lew went running with the dogs, and I came up to write, but I think I'll go back down again. It's the end of a beautiful Sabbath day. The way they all should be.

'Bye for now. Hope Lew is still there.

11:13 P.M.

Far away on the north side of the lake, I could hear Lew laughing and the dogs barking. I was so glad he was still out that my heart "wafted" around inside my chest. Don't you love that word?

He was surprised to see me still sitting where he'd left me, and he and the dogs just crumpled down around me. They were all panting and semi-wet where they'd splashed into the rippling little waves. One dog stood up and shook all over me.

I pulled away from his shower right into Lew's arms. He held me there so the dog could spray me even more . . . we laughed for a second; then he reached over and kissed me. It was so sweet and gentle and soft, like nothing I'd ever felt before in my life, like I was in Paradise or something. I had one freak-out moment when the thought passed through my mind that he didn't really know how to kiss; then it wafted away in the moonlight. That was not true. Collin was the one who didn't know how to kiss. After a few minutes, we got up and walked back to the house, hand in hand. Life will never be the same.

Want to hear a wonderful and sacred secret, Self? I couldn't possibly, ever in the world, share it with anybody but *you!* For the first time in my life I really and honestly, truly love a guy. I—with all my heart, and forever—love Lew Fullmark.

Little Lew Fullmark Jr.
Baby Nancy Fullmark

Oh, doesn't that have a beautiful ring to it.

The moon is so bright I could almost take my book out and write by its light. I would, except Uncle Bill asked us not to go out alone at night because there are a lot of wild animals around. I forgot to remind Lew of that when he went running with the dogs. Oh, I am so glad that nothing happened to him! I don't know what I'd ever do if anything happened to Lew. He's been the biggest, brightest part of my so-far forever.

Sincerely,
Mrs. Nancy Fullmark
No.
With best regards,
Mrs. Lewis K. Fullmark

Monday, June 11

8:22 A.M.

I don't know what's wrong with me. I feel so icky I could hardly force myself out of bed. I can hear the gaggle out running and playing by the lake. Lew and Uncle Bill are putting up two big car-tire swings, and it looks so fun and it sounds so fun that my insides are dying to go down, but my body just feels like it can't make it. I hope I'm not coming down with something. I can't be! I won't get sick now! Please, please, nature, that's not fair! All my life I've had allergies and asthma and respiratory problems, and I'll gladly have them when I get home, but please, please, not here, not now!

I dressed slowly as a little old lady, and I've taken my breathing excercises, so I feel some better. I hope the gaggle won't notice. What if I look as crappy as I feel? No, no, I can't do that. I'll feel better as soon as I see Lew. An answer to prayer. There he is, swinging on the tire swing like an angel flying through the air. Now he's Tarzan beating his chest and yelling. Oh, I do feel better. Thank you, God. Oh, thank you very much. I want to go do it too. Me Jane. Me go down to Tarzan.

11:20 A.M.

Late this afternoon we leave to go home. I don't want to ever leave this place. It's where my life really started. Lew and I steal kisses whenever we can elude the gaggle. Behind the big rock, up by the point, out behind the boathouse, once even in the hall. They're usually just little pecks, but it's a fun game.

Please, day, last a long, long time. Don't ever end.

Tuesday, June 12

12:01 P.M.—Home

I'll never forget our trip. Lew and I went out in the canoe together before we left. It tips over so easily that Uncle Bill won't let more than two go out at a time, and then we have to stay really close to the shore.

When we were beyond the point, away from the house, he stopped, pulled the oars in and told me that I'm as big a part of his life as he is of mine. I wonder if he's ever written "Mr. and Mrs. Lewis Fullmark," but, of course, I didn't ask him. I don't think boys do silly things like girls do. I wonder if he's ever thought it, though.

Lew remembers the first time he kissed me, when we were about six. He even remembers where it was—at his house by their volleyball court. We went in and told his family that we were going to get married. Then I got on my bike and rode home. I'm so glad he remembers. I didn't think he did.

He even remembers the CKH ring that I wore on a chain around my neck. My grandmother gave it to me when I was seven, and after she died, it was like having part of her close to me. Lew even remembered that the CKH stands for CHOOSE KINDNESS AND HONOR! He said he envied me having the ring and wished his grandma had given him something like that instead of a—he looked embarrassed—little locket that had belonged to his great-grandmother that had a picture of her on one side and a picture of him, "her most beautiful great-grandchild," on the other.

He giggled, and I giggled with him. "Were you really her favorite, most beautiful great-grandchild?" I asked.

He squeezed me and slopped a little kiss on my cheek, "No, That's the family joke, because by the time I was born, Great-Grandma was blind." He looked far away into the past. "I suspect my silly brothers started that rumor."

I looked adoringly into his face. "I don't think so. I know it's true," I said with all my heart.

Anyway, I took my CKH ring and chain off my neck and offered it to him. "I don't know of anyone I've ever known who is as kind and honorable as you."

His eyes got moist as he accepted it, and he said, "And will you wear my great-grandmother's locket? It's silly because it's got a picture of me in it when I was two years old. My hair was white as cotton and curly and fluffy as a little girl's."

I reached over to kiss him, and we almost turned the canoe over. It was pretty spooky scary while he tried to get it straightened up, but he never did let go of the CKH ring.

Oh, what a beautiful day. It has been by far the most beautiful day of my life. THE BEGINNING OF A FUTURE THAT IS GOING TO BE MORE GLORIOUS THAN HAS EVER BEEN KNOWN BY MANKIND SINCE THE BEGINNING OF THE EARTH . . . AS WELL AS ALL THE OTHER CREATIONS OF INFINITY.

Wednesday, June 13

4:15 P.M.

I must have a bug because I'm so tired and worn out all the time. I seem to be always pushing, and for the first time in my life I'm glad that Mom won't let me go out much at night except for something special.

8:01 P.M.

I can't believe I haven't written in you for so long,
but I've been *so* busy and *so* happy and *SO TIRED!*
But I *won't,* I can't, let anybody know how hard it is
for me to keep up, especially Mom, because then she
really would make me go to Arizona with Dad. July
Fourth I felt like a fizzle cracker while everybody
else was a firecracker.

The gaggle is always together. Sometimes I get
mad because Lew and I have so little time alone, but
I guess that's good in a way because Kelly Karson
and Belinda Carter both got pregnant this year. I
heard Belinda had an abortion; I could never, ever,
never do that! And Kelly, I don't know what she's
going to do. Whatever it is, it's going to be really
hard, because she's just fifteen and Roger is just sixteen. I heard they were using condoms too. That's
pretty hairy-scary.

Only once have Lew and I come close; then he
made me promise *to God* that we'd either keep it
cool till we're seventeen, when we'd talk about it
again, or we'd quit seeing each other altogether. That
scared me so much that I'll never let him or me get
carried away again. I can't give him up. No way in
this world could I ever exist without him.

I've stopped playing in the band. Last week we
played in a parade for the Big Pine Centennial, and I
got so tired and out of breath that half the time I was
just pretending to play. I guess I've taken on more
than I can handle. Anyway, I told Mr. Miller that in
the fall I'd have to give up a scholarly project or
band, and I thought it would be better for me, in the

long run, to give up band now. He agreed, thank goodness, so I'm off that hook!

I hope I'm not going to start having horrible allergy and respiratory problems like I did when I was a little kid. I thought I'd outgrown most of that, but maybe not, or maybe I'm just run-down. I hope that's it.

Thursday, July 19

9:43 P.M.

It's been two weeks, and I'm getting a little scared. I have this nagging, heavy-bag-of-sand-in-my-chest kind of feeling that doesn't seem to want to go away. I'm taking all my medication and eating right and excercising, and I'm under *no stress* at all. In fact, life has never been so smooth and ice-creamy. Mom and I are getting along better than we ever have, and she's letting Lew come over some nights to help me with my math. She's even dumber than I am about geometry, which is funny because I've seen her work on millions of dollars' projections for a building, with no sweat at all. I'm trying to catch up on math this summer so I can be a straight A student in the fall—*I wish!*

Saturday, July 21

P.M.

A bunch of us went to the water slides today. It was fun for a while; then I got tired and watched all the other kids. None of them, not one, seems to tire as quickly as I do. I try to cover it up and say it's my period and all like that, but I feel like it's getting

worse. But, of course, it isn't! I'm just being paranoid! I've always been smaller and slighter than the
rest of the girls my age.

Lew says he likes it that I'm not a tomboy like
Red. He reminded me of the time at school when we
went on our biology project to the lake, and he carried me back to the bus on his back. Big deal—*I* carried the frogs in the bottles. I told him that I was
doing my part . . . but I felt funny then and I feel fun-
nier now.

Wednesday, July 25

5:59 P.M.

Mom said I was looking peaked, so she made an
appointment with the doctor without my knowing it.
Dr. Talbert, who brought me into the world, and who
has thumped me on my chest since I can remember
and has given me shots and stuff, thumped and listened some more, then gave me some vitamins and
told me to cut down on some of my activities. He
also made me promise I'd eat my veggies and drink
my milk, etc., like I was a little kid. I promised to
keep him and Mom happy. Actually, I'd do anything
to make myself feel really good again. It's kind of
like I'm a light bulb, and I used to be 100 watts and
now I'm just 40 or 50 or 5. It's a strange feeling,
which I didn't try to explain to Dr. Talbert. He
wouldn't have understood. It doesn't really even
make sense to me. I still give off light and stuff, and
no one else seems to notice it *that* much, but I do! I
want all the light back!

Dear Self:

I need to talk to you. I really do. I'm so glad I've got you. I need to see what went wrong. Mom was out of town again on business, and Lew came over to study with me. It was so quiet and nice, with only the three of us there, me and him and Imperical. I told him about Imperical—well, not *all* about Imperical, but the good parts.

After we'd studied, we went out on the terrace and ate Oreos and drank milk out of the carton and tried to count the stars. We were both lying on one lounge, and as we counted we got more and more involved until we . . . we almost did . . . Then Lew jumped up, and he was so mad at me I thought he was going to dump me over the rail or something. But he said he was really more mad at himself. He pulled me to my feet and dragged me out of the apartment and down the street. I was too afraid to speak, even though I knew he'd never do anything mean . . . I hoped . . .

Silently, he walked so fast to Acorn, then down to Magnolia, that I had to run to keep up. He was holding me so tight by the upper arm that it hurt, but I didn't dare say anything.

At Magnolia and 33rd there was a big church of some kind, and Lew dragged me in. "Is this your church?" I whispered.

"No," he whispered back, "it's not *my* church or *your* church. It's God's church." He dragged me down the aisle and pushed me down to my knees on a prayer bench. "Now you and I are really going to make a promise to God that we won't . . ." He didn't finish, but I knew. And I did promise. I really did. I sincerely and honestly and with every fiber of myself did.

Lew didn't speak to me on the way back to my apartment. He just stopped at the front door and said coldly, "We won't see each other for three weeks."

I wanted to cry and fall at his feet and beg, but I didn't. I was probably the aggressor. I felt so lost and forsaken. What if I had explained about—no, never! Lew must *never* know about Collin.

I hope he meant that after three weeks we can see each other again. Did he? He had to! I can't live without Lew. I don't want to.

Saturday, July 28

5:53 P.M.

Lew sent me the sweetest, longest letter. It was under our door when I got home from Mom's office, where I'm doing a little "go for" work. I was in deep, deep, almost unbearable pain because he has been avoiding me. I couldn't have stood it if he had dumped me. Being trashed once was all I could stand. No way could I have stood it twice. Anyway, Lew's letter made me so sad that an adult would, could, never understand or feel the sadness. He told me that when his parents had said that they were going to divorce, right then and there he made a commitment, solemn as it could be, that he would never have sex until he was married. He had heard that word *sex* over and over between his parents, and even though he was only ten and didn't really understand what sex really meant at that point, he knew it was the thing that had destroyed the family. His dad was having sex with other women, and with his mom sick and all, it was really dreadful, *dreadful, DREAD-FUL!* He wanted to somehow make *them* feel the *pain!* As it was, they seemed to feel only the anger.

Lew is so self-disciplined and mature. He's all the things I want to be, and he understands things so perfectly; his thoughts and feelings are exactly like mine. It's like he's reading my mind and soul, especially when he said, "I wondered why my dad didn't realize that when he was being unfaithful to his wife, he was also being unfaithful to his kids." Lew wondered how he could be so smart and not know that. I felt like he was talking about me and my dad, and my wet tears joined his tears that had dried up on the paper.

Lew told me if I wanted to dump him he'd understand, but that's how he had always felt and always would feel! He said that maybe waiting for marriage wasn't for me, and he'd understand. He knew that lots of kids were doing it, and always had and always would, but that he had his free agency as much as they did. He had *committed* to be more *future*-oriented than *now*-oriented!

I am so proud of Lew, so amazed by his brilliance and his decisions. I want to stroke his head and hold his hand, to tell him I love him and that I feel the exact same way, but that will have to wait for *three* weeks!!! THREE LONG WEEKS!!! THREE FOREVER WEEKS!!!

Sunday, July 29—Eighteen More Days

Lew smiles when he sees me and stuff, but he's just friendly like I was any old body. I want to go kneel at his feet and beg him to let it be like it was, but I've got to learn to be self-disciplined too, to have some control over my emotions as well as my life. Chips, neither one of us had any protection that night that we almost ... if we had ... I might ... at this very moment ... be *pregnant* like Kelly and Belinda. Oh, horrors ... pain ... strain ... Mom ... Dad ... Lew's family ... school ... marriage ... abortion? No, no, I won't even think about the A word.

I knew I didn't want to with *&+=*, but I thought that maybe when I was seventeen or eighteen, with protection I would. It seems like everybody does. *EVERYBODY, THAT IS, EXCEPT ME AND LEW!* Lew and me! Oh, I love that boy so much. I love him and admire him and respect him and revere him, and want to enjoy his forever company forever, and I *WILL* BE WORTHY OF HIM! I REALLY, TRULY, HONESTLY WILL BE! I WILL MAKE HIM FOREVER PROUD OF ME! I WILL PREPARE MYSELF TO BE HIS FOREVER WIFE! I PROMISE! I PROMISE! I PROMISE! I PROMISED BEFORE IN THE CHURCH, AND I RENEW THAT SACRED, EVERLASTING PROMISE NOW!

August 1—Fifteen More Days

I've got some kind of inflammation or something in my chest again. I keep hacking and spitting up phlegm. It's nauseating. Sometimes I almost choke myself before I can get to the bathroom and flush the toilet while I gag and spit. It's disgusting. I've seen old men do it in the park, and I wanted to cover my eyes and hold my hands over my ears even then.

Sunday, August 5

I'm using everything: faith, a crystal, a voodoo good-luck-good-health doll and mind over body. I wonder what Lew will do and say when he sees me. Is it possible that I look as bad as I feel? Oh, I do hope not.

Tuesday, August 7—Nine More Days

I'm missing everything.

I've been sick over a week, and I'm not getting better. I hate to admit it, but I think I'm really getting worse. I can cover from Mom, but I really want to be well in a week. In only a week and two more days and ... Heaven will open its pearly gates ... I will see him, touch him ... I wonder where ... When will he kiss me again? Will he ever? It's all right if he doesn't. I will still love him for infinity, no matter what.

Saturday, August 11—Five More Days

I'm feeling a lot better. I think my antihistamine just kicked in ... or maybe I'm just so excited and happy that my immune system is happy and excited too. I don't care which, I'm just happy and excited about everything—air, grass, sky, doing dishes, cleaning my room, helping Mom, etc., etc., etc. I'm really, really, really trying my best for the first time in my life for me and for Lew. Lew is an A student. He is the Student Body President and important in everything that *is* important at school. I want to make him proud of me. I want to be the very best ME I can be. Knowing Lew has changed my whole life. My whole forever life. I am getting disciplined and controlled like he wants me to be. I'm doing the things I *ought* to do before the things I *want* to do! It's a very mature concept that makes me feel very mature.

Thursday, August 16

5:15 A.M.—THE DAY

I woke up at five o'clock and Imperical and I have been out on the terrace singing our hearts out. I hum and then he hums. He seems to know what a sacred day this is for me. Joy to the world and everything in it and around it.

Never was a day so beautiful, a sky so blue, clouds so white, flower fragrance so sweet, me so happy! I can't wait. I cannot wait! Lew will . . . what?

6:30 P.M.

Today was everything I dreamed and hoped and prayed it would be. Lew and I had lunch at a little table in the back of the A to Z cafeteria. The gaggle left us alone because I told them we had had a fight and were now going to make up. I'm not sure they would understand our true situation, even if I could tell them.

We were both a little embarrassed; we, who had never had any trouble talking, who in fact often both talked at once, spent a lot of time just looking at each other and at our hands.

Lew said his mom would like to have me over Saturday for a barbecue. I know that he had arranged it, because we had talked about not spending so much time *alone* together. But it would be fun. I hadn't seen Mike, Lew's big baby-sitting brother, in months. Maybe he needs to baby-sit us again, huh? NO!

We've made solemn, sacred decisions and commitments, and we'll keep them. When we have a class reunion fifty years from now, we'll still be together with all of our bratty, spoiled, well-loved, *definitely wanted* kids. I wonder if he thinks about things like this. Am I weird?

Saturday, August 18

10:17 P.M.

What a beautiful, special day. Lew came by, and we walked over to his house. It's almost eight blocks away, but we cut through old Mr. Cutler's backyard—making it a lot less.

Today it seemed like we'd never had a problem of any kind. We didn't mention it, in fact, I didn't even think about it after the first couple of minutes. I don't think he did either. The *NOW* was too incredible to worry about, or even be concerned with, the past.

I was surprised to see Lew's mother in a wheelchair and looking all sort of unhinged or something. She put her bony little arms out to me, and I went over and hugged her. She's so scrawny and shrunken now. I remember her in my head as a big, tall, stately woman, sort of always laughing or talking and in charge, except when Lew's dad was there. Then she relaxed and let him take over. I always liked that.

Kyle and Mike came in, and after saying wonderful, flattering things to me that made me feel coy and blushing, Mike started teasing me and Lew and pretending that we were the obnoxious little brats he used to have to tend. When I spilled barbecue sauce, he jumped up and down and yelled, "I'm gonna tell Mama. I'm gonna tell." And when Lew went to get a second cup of punch, he did it again. "Mama, Lew's drinking all the punch. Lew's drinking all the punch, Mama. Punch him out, Mama. I'll help you."

Kyle just sat by his mom and laughed. They were having so much fun that I decided Mike could tease me forever and I wouldn't get mad.

After dinner, the three boys went swimming. I wouldn't have gotten in the pool with those three ruffians for anything. They were diving under each other, trying to pull the top one down and screaming and laughing and splashing like three crazy people.

Occasionally, one or the other would pretend to be drowning and yell, "Mama, come get me. Save me . . . me. Save me . . ." Or, "Nancy, I'm going down for the last time . . . help . . . glug . . . glug . . . glug." Then they'd go down and blow up bubbles.

I felt like I was six years old and at my first really big birthday party. I hadn't known that grown-ups and almost-grown-ups and kids could have so much fun together. This was the way life should be, except there should be a father there, and the mother not sick.

Now I knew exactly what I want my future, future, future to be. Lew feels exactly the same.

Sunday, August 19

I woke up so sick that I could hardly call for Mom. When she came, I just hugged her, trying not to pass out. I couldn't breathe. I couldn't even get up to get my medicine. She got it and my inhaler, and I felt some better.

I guess I just overdid yesterday.

I went to the bathroom, and I'm glad Lew went with his family to see some relatives out in the country. I certainly wouldn't want him to see me! I look so hollow-eyed and pale. I guess I better spend the rest of the day in bed trying to get myself well for when school starts pretty soon. I can't miss school. I CAN'T! I won't!

Monday, August 20

When I first got up, I looked like I'd just stepped out of the Addams Family's haunted house, but after plastering on the makeup, I was passable for a human being.

Lew's brother Kyle had car trouble, so they had to stay over. In a way I'm glad, because it takes more energy than I've got just to breathe.

Tuesday, August 21

All is well again. The gaggle brought beat-up, sloppy-wrapped gifts to El's to celebrate because Lew and I are back together again. A bottle of glue so we'd "stick to each other"... a big candy-heart cookie that had been broken in half and frosted together, with a "How sweet it is" sign ... a rubber band "so you'll always snap back where you belong." It was all so fun that a lot of other kids got in on it too, giving us crazy advice about how not to break up again. We laughed at it, but we didn't need it. We've got our forever act together for keeps.

None of us wanted to leave the party; it was so much fun.

Wednesday, August 22

8:17 A.M.

Tomorrow is my doctor's appointment. I hope he can change my meds or give me something different, because I really am draggin' my wagon.

Thursday, August 23

7:50 P.M.—Hospital

I can't believe it. After lunch Mom took me for my appointment, and after the usual thumping and stuff, Dr. Talbert said he wanted me to go directly to the hospital. I couldn't even go home to get my toothbrush. Apparently he thinks I've got pneumonia, but I don't think so. I don't feel *THAT* bad.

Saturday, August 25

6:30 P.M.—Written on a Paper Bag

I've had X-rays and all the garbage in their books, lights in my ears and nose and a tube down my throat and bloodletting and pinches in my stomach, etc., etc., etc.

They're going to make me stay another night. What a dawdle.

8:29 P.M.

Lew came by just before visiting hours were over. He was so worried about me that it made my heart flutter. I told him that they couldn't even find anything wrong with me. I'm sure I'll go home tomorrow.

Lew kissed me so tenderly when the nurse left that it has stamped a picture and feeling in my soul that I will never forget, even when we're old and gray fogies.

Sunday, August 26

9:18 A.M.

Mom came by this morning and said she thought maybe I'd like to go to nice, hot, dry Arizona for a while to clear up my lungs. She thought wrong! WRONG! WRONG! There's no way *anything* could make me leave the gaggle, ESPECIALLY THE *GANDER* PART OF THE GAGGLE! I wish I could tell her how much in love I am. How my love isn't like hers. It's not going to break up after a few years. It's like forever, for eternities, for infinity. Lew and I were together in the heavens before we came here, and we're going to be together in the heavens after we die. I don't think she would understand that; not many people would. Lew and I do. That is enough! Isn't that funny, when I'm not even really religious . . . I mean I don't go to Mass every day and like that, or hardly ever for that matter, but there's just something inside me that makes me comfortable with thoughts like Heaven and forever. Like there's something that makes me uncomfortable with the kids who can't use a sentence without half of it being filthy or sexy. I know lots and lots of kids at school and the mall are full of it . . . and they do it . . . and they have a right, but . . . not us.

NOTHING IS MORE BORING THAN A HOSPITAL. I'm sure I'll be released today. I'm feeling so much better. I guess I just needed some rest.

9:34 A.M.

I hate these crazy beds where your feet are squooshed flat. Nobody's feet bend that way! I got up and pulled the sheets out at the bottoms so I could lie with my toes pointing *up* like they want to. Poor little cramped toesies. And food. . . . I'd die for a pizza.

10:10 A.M.

Mom just came in again and said Dr. Talbert had asked her to come. Wow. Like I'm going home . . . home . . . home. I'm outta here.

9:01 P.M.—Home

I'm in a nightmare. I'm going to wake up any minute now. I've got to. It repeats over and over! I can see Dr. Talbert's face with his eyes all glazed up, and Mom looking like she's a marble statue. Her hand on mine even feels cold and hard like one. We can sense something is really wrong when Dr. Talbert keeps telling us how great we are and stuff, like he can't really get out what he wants to say. Then he slowly tells me that my blood samples have come back, and I have . . . . *the HIV virus!* His mouth keeps moving, but I can't hear words anymore. I can't feel; I can't think. I may be dumb and young and naive, but I'm not stupid. Someone's made the most horrible of horrible mistakes. How could *I* have . . . AIDS? The word is like all the bitterness in the world on my tongue, then spreading throughout my body. I've never had a blood transfusion; I've never used a dirty needle. I've never had . . . I looked at Mom with panic . . . I was *raped*. But that couldn't be it either, could it? Could it happen the first time?

From far off in the distance, I could hear myself sobbing, frightened, little-girl, almost-baby sobs. They wouldn't stop. They will never stop!

I don't even remember Mom bringing me home and putting me to bed. Dr. Talbert probably gave me something. I hope he gave Mom something too.

Thoughts run through my brain crashing into each other, scrambling around like eggs in my hot skull. What if Lew and I had? I think *I* would have! I'm almost sure *I* would have! If Lew hadn't made us stop . . . I wanted to soooooo much. If we had, would *he* now have AIDS too? He probably would have, because neither one of us had any protection. Or would he? Do people get it every time? There's so much I need to know. I must know!

Thank you, God, for making Lew strong.

What if after *&+=- I hadn't met Lew, and I'd become just another one of the school whores, passing *it* around like M&M's?

Oh, please, please, please, I need another sleeping pill. I really do!

1:30 A.M.

I've got to face it. . . . I AM GOING TO DIE. . . . I'm not going to have a career, or a husband or a family. My heart is bursting. I am *never* going to have Lew. He'll have to find someone else to take my place. . . . I hope, oh, I do hope she'll love him as much as I do, and for forever!

6:57 P.M.

It's become *real!* Too real! We had a counselor here for a couple of hours. I guess she helped. At least now I know what I can and can't do to *protect Mom!* I hadn't realized that I could be an endangerment to her, to everybody.

Missy, the counselor, kept saying I *wasn't;* then she'd tell me something that would tell me I was! No. 1: HIV is carried almost exclusively through blood and semen. Okay, well, we don't have to worry about semen—but blood . . . ummmm. I suspect sometimes in the past I've used Mom's toothbrush because I was just too lazy or hurried to take her blue brush off and put my yellow one on the electric toothbrush machine, and sometimes I do have bleeding gums if I have canker sores or something.

"HIV is not a fragile virus and can live up to seven days in body fluids." What does that mean? It's all so complicated. What if I splatter on the toilet seat during my period, and Mom has an open rash on her bum? What do I do with used Tampax? What if I cough hard and spit up a little blood with the phlegm, like I sometimes do? I need Missy to come back. Now! Not tomorrow—now! Now! Now!

12:42 A.M.

I'm beginning to see the really black side of AIDS that everyone tries to hide. Guess I'll just pretend that everything is okay with me. Then I'll die.

7:15 A.M.

I called El and told her my dad was sick and I was going to stay with him for a while. He really isn't sick, but I have to get away to get my beans together. It was hard to convince El that I was doing the right thing, but I did. She said she'd get the word around and they'd all write me.

I hated to tell such a big, black lie, but I can't handle seeing the kids right now, especially Lew. I really can't. What would I say? What would I do? Maybe I'll die right away, and I won't have to do anything.

7 P.M.

Missy, the counselor, came and spent most of the afternoon with Mom and me. I wanted her to answer a lot of questions I had written down, but we started talking about *&=-+, and my questions sort of got brushed away.

Missy and Mom both want me to report *&=-+ to the police. At first I resisted. I don't want everybody in the world to know what happened to me, how stupid I was, how gullible, but then they got me to thinking about little Margie and . . . well . . . I guess I'll do what I *ought* to do instead of what I want to do. Actually, I really, truly do want to do it now that I've considered it! The thought of little Margie having AIDS makes me sick. How may others have there been? The thought is worse than a nightmare.

Thursday, August 30

8:10 A.M.

It's a strange thing, but thinking about other people and trying to help them is making me feel better. At least now I have a positive reason for existing.

A policewoman is coming over this afternoon with Missy, and we're going to get at least one menace off the streets. That makes me happy, and I didn't think I'd every be happy again. Well, I'm not *really* happy, but at least I'm up to about one-half millionth on a scale from one to ten. For the last few days I've been about minus 300 million.

4:26 P.M.

Janie Dee, the police lady, and Missy really made me feel important. They say if more kids would report—they called them predators—they could stop at least some of them. I looked the word up in the dictionary, because it didn't sound bad enough to me. *Predator:* one who plunders, loots, wastes, destroys, preys upon, etc. But no word could really be bad enough for ... him!!! How? Why? Why could he have done this to me? Why didn't he just kill me and get it over with in a hurry?

Missy said he "preyed" upon me like a cat toys with a mouse. Chips, I can't believe that I once thought of *&=-+ as the most beautiful creation that God had ever made. I thought he was the most personable, the most verbal, the most honorable ... everything. What a fool. What a stupid, dumb, idiotic, birdbrained, empty-headed, mixed-up fool. He is Satan incarnate.

A police artist is coming over in the morning to

sketch him as I see him. That should be easy, because his picture is burned into my brain like he was standing right here.

Isn't it funny how things come in handy when you never think they would? When Mom and I visited her aunt Thelma on her ranch in Idaho, while Mom lazed around the cabin and read and stuff, Aunt Thelma and I took the horses out on long trips. Always, she brought pads and pastels and stuff along, and she'd draw beautifully, and I'd try . . . not too successfully . . . if you remember, Self, and I'm positively sure you do. At least at first they were bad, but I got better, didn't I, at remembering details anyway?

10:27 P.M.

I wonder why God made the nights so long. I can't sleep, I can't concentrate on TV, I can't write, I can't read . . . I can only think and think and relive . . . and relive . . . and suffer.

12:03 A.M.

I've decided to at least do something constructive! I will give the police sketch person a description of *&=-+ that they will not believe possible. And all because of Aunt Thelma and her tutoring me the miracle of really *LOOKING AND SEEING!* It was wonderful, finding the hidden little miracles after she had shown me how. By Indian Paint Brush Falls, she had me look down into the crack in the rocks to find the tiniest, most fragile, different-color flowers I had ever seen. She said many people had passed that way for centuries, and probably few had seen the unearthly fragileness and other-world shades of color.

When we found things like that or Indian writings

on bare canyon walls, or even unusual rock forma-
tions, she would have me look at the thing until I had
absolutely imprinted it on my mind. Then I would
describe it to her as if she were blind, remembering
each tiniest little color and texture, width and length
and everything else in relationship to everything
around it.

I'm so grateful to Aunt Thelma for this wonderful,
perfect reproduction album of pictures I have in my
mind. Sometimes we'd turn our backs on the sacredly
special thing we'd just seen, and we'd paint it from
memory. It was a fun game, me trying to find things
she'd left out in her paintings and her trying to find
things I'd left out in mine! It was fun, and it taught
me something I've used many times since, but always for good before . . . maybe this will be for good
too. Maybe after I've re-created *&=-+ for the police,
I'll be able to completely erase him. I wonder if it's
possible to do that. I think I'll call Aunt Thelma first
thing in the morning. No, I can't do that; how could
I ever explain *&=-+ to someone as "unspotted from
the world" as Aunt Thelma? I don't know where I
heard or read that phrase, but it really describes her.
She was the one who taught me that people who use
crude and vulgar words only do it because they don't
have the vocabulary or the desire to describe things
as they truly are. She printed that so indelibly in my
mind that I usually automatically don't . . . well, most
of the time I don't.

3:42 A.M.

I've drawn a colored-pencil sketch of Coll-
Throw-Up that I think, when the drawing guy does it,
and I give him a few more suggestions about size and

stuff, will create a reproduction that will be almost lifelike. This one is so much like him that I can't work on it anymore. It's already spotted with tears.

Friday, August 31

11:49 A.M.

Missy and the policy sketch artist came at nine o'clock. They both loved the sketch I'd made of Throw-Up. Officer Williams had some books and stuff and by the time he'd finished his picture, it was almost like a colored photograph. I could even tell the policeman how much taller Throw-Up was than me, and from the body sizes in the book I found one that could have been his brother, or him.

As soon as Officer Williams had finished the sketch, the bottom fell out of my energy container, whatever it is, and so they both left. Missy said that she'd be back tomorrow to answer some of the important questions that I've got to ask her but we've never had time for. I hope she knows the answers. I do hope so! I need to know everything about AIDs.

Saturday, September 1

Noon

I just fixed myself a peanut butter and banana and jelly sandwich, but I only took one bite. Nothing tastes good anymore, or looks good, or feels good. I wonder if I'll ever get out of this funk. I am a basket case! I don't want to die. I really don't. I'm scared. It isn't fair. I want to live to be an old, wrinkled-up little lady who knits things and paints and stuff, and has lots of kids and grandkids hanging around and a husband who is true and faithful . . . and dependable . . . like Lew. I mean . . . I hope . . . I wish . . . really Lew. But none of that can ever be now.

From here on, it's just death and me trying to stare each other down. Oh, I can't handle that. I'm just being morbid and self-centered and paranoid and all the other negative self-serving stuff I don't want to be. I've got to be more . . . more . . . I wish I knew what.

2 A.M.

I don't know why I'm thinking about school starting . . . I'm not even sure I'll live to graduate from high school. I wonder how long it will be till I . . . Will I just get tired and then more tired and then I'll just go to sleep forever?

I've got to get some more of those books about people seeing lights and tunnels of warmth and beauty, and having someone all white and shiny come to take them from here to there, wherever *there* is. I read once, a long time ago, a book called *Return to Tomorrow,* or something. I wonder if I could get it at the library. I suspect I'll look at it a lot differently now.

3:24 A.M.

I *really* don't want to die. I love my bed. I love my room. I love my mom. I love my dad. I love Imperical. I love to hear him twitter early in the morning before it's quite light. I usually wake up to that soft, wonderful belonging sound. I don't want to leave it ever! Ever! Ever! I'm scared . . . I'm really scared! I'm not absolutely positive there is that Heaven that I want so desperately to be there. Oh, please, please, God, let there be a Heaven for me to go to. I don't want to just be a poor, lost, lonely soul wandering through space forever. That's stupid ... that's dumb ... that's morbid ... and I used to be sooooooo happy. I can hardly remember those days.

Tuesday, September 4—I think

(But who cares? One day just runs into another.)

Guess what? My old 7th grade teacher who used to live next door, was in the neighborhood, and dropped by to say hi. I think she's psychic! She said she'd dreamed about me. She tried to make me laugh and stuff. Maybe she'll have to teach me *that* all over again too. I hope she can.

3:09 P.M.

Officer Williams came over, and it was really strange. I don't think he hypnotized me, but he just talked quietly and had me relax all my muscles and nerves and stuff. He'd pulled the shades on the windows and turned the lights down, and it was quiet and restful and a safe feeling. After a little he asked me to remember all I could about Throw-Up's car and stuff. He even calls *him* that now; so do Missy and Mom. Anyway, I don't think I did too well on that, but when he quietly, slowly, caringly asked me to recall every detail that Throw-Up had said about his personal life or past, I remembered that one day, when we were sitting by the lake throwing rocks in and talking about my Philomena Farnsworth Junior High and what a funny name that was, he said that his junior high was just plain old Abraham Lincoln Junior High. At least mine was different.

Officer Williams seemed happy about that, although I don't know what great good it would be;

there must be nine hundred Abraham Lincoln what-evers in wherever.

Wednesday, September 5

10:10 A.M.

Officer Williams called and said there were only a few Abraham Lincoln Junior High schools and that he was going to get me all their yearbooks, and I'd go through the pictures to see if I recognized Throw-Up. He seemed pretty sure I would. I hope he's right.

Thursday, September 6

3:30 P.M.

I can't believe it, but I think I'm feeling better. At least the sun seemed warm today, and Mom brought me some raspberries, which I snarfed down like a starving person.

Missy comes nearly every day. She's convincing me that I've gotta get on with my life. She's even telling me that I can get my beans together and be a real person again. Maybe I can get up and get out! Go back to school again. Laugh, play, work, feel . . . at least some things besides pain. Do *you* think I can, Self? *Your* opinion is important to me, you know. Okay, if you say I can, I CAN, AND I WILL, AND I SHOULD, AND I SHALL. SO THERE. HA . . . ha, ha, ha.

7:15 P.M.

I felt so good, I had Mom take a walk with me. We just went around the complex a few times, but we had fun. We played Follow the Leader and skipped and hopped, and ran and jumped and did all the silly little things we did when I was young. I guess past tense is right. I'll never by young again, or will I? Ummm, maybe I will. Missy says being positive is the biggest part of my recovery.

Monday, September 10

10:30 A.M.

I haven't been able to read the letters the gaggle sent to me in care of my dad, and he shipped back to me. They just made me feel more guilty and like the biggest liar in the universe, but now ... well, here goes. I hope I don't drown out my bedroom with my tears and have my bed floating down the hall.

One ... two ... three ... rip.

11:47 A.M.

I guess I had never realized until this very minute how precious and wonderful and special and, well, almost sacred—*no, really sacred*—friends are. Their love covers me and protects me and warms me like the soft little "banky" security blanket I had when I was a baby. I remember, when I was about three, dragging it around everywhere I went and sucking my thumb. Each finger had a flavor: orange, strawberry, raspberry, peanut butter, and lime. Suck-suck-suck. I can still taste those wonderful flavors. My mind is flooded with sweet, sweet old memories as well as the caring ones in the letters. *Everyone* misses me and wants me back! Lew said a piece of the jigsaw puzzle of his life is missing with me gone, and that's the piece right in the left-hand corner of his chest. Isn't that beautiful? How am I going to handle us?

1 A.M.

Once Mom told me the story of *Gone with the Wind*. She said Scarlett O'Hara always said, when things were bad, "I'll worry about that tomorrow." I think that saying is going to become a big part of my life from here on.

Awwww . . . I just yawned and stretched and realized that I'm very relaxed and sleepy. Isn't that delicious? For some time now I've only slept when I was exhausted.

> Good night, nice friends.
> Good night, nice Mom.
> Good night, nicer-than-nice Lew.
> Good night, Dearer-than-Dear Self.

Friday, September 14

8 A.M.

I got up early and fixed Mom's breakfast. Aren't I nice? She didn't want to lie for me, but she finally consented to call El and tell her I'd be home tomorrow. Isn't she the best mom ever? I'm so lucky to have her, and I appreciate her soooooooo much, even though sometimes I don't act like it.

I've got to hurry and do my homework before my home schoolteacher gets here. She's nice, but she'll never take the place of the gaggle. They are so . . . I can't even think of words fantastic enough. I am so lucky, lucky, lucky. God must love me.

Saturday, September 15

4:30 P.M.

I met El and Red at the mall. We had lunch at Pizza Heaven, and it was *that*. They had so much to tell me, they were both talking at once, and I was trying to listen to each of them, and we were giggling and spilling and choking on our food. The people at the next table gave us dirty looks, and we all just turned up our noses and pretended we were better than they were—so we could do what we wanted even it if was nutty and childish and stuff. I WANT TO BE CHILDISH! I NEED TO BE CHILDISH! I DESERVE TO BE CHILDISH! . . . Because I don't really know *how long* I've got to be whatever.

Oh, forget that pity-party stuff, Self. We are going to live like we've got forever! Promise? Promise you'll help me? Okay! Good! Thanks!

El says Dorie has a boyfriend that her parents don't know about. After I begged for about an hour, they told me it was Fred Simmons. I don't know about him. He's in high school and I'm sooo worried. But he was in ninth when we were in seventh, and he seemed like a good kid. . . . ha. Oh, how sad. Will I forever, from now on, be jaded and mistrusting and negative?

Lew's gone to his cousin's for the weekend, and I'm really kind of glad. At least that give me a little more time to decide what . . . how . . . if. Life is so confusing that I guess I'll just wait and "worry about tomorrow tomorrow." Okay? Okay!

El and Red and I are going to the movies tonight.

We've all seen what's playing three times, but we're going again. We all love the music as well as the tenderness of the story. The only problem is that I feel dangerous now. Oh, that's dumb. I don't make sense now more than I *do* make sense!

11:10 P.M.

We couldn't get into the movie we wanted, so we just went to the nearest one. It was soooooooo old and silly and childish and dumb. We all laughed until we cried and choked and beat on each other. You could hardly hear the dialogue, and when you could, the whole audience was talking along with it.

Hey, I really had fun. It was like the old days. I didn't think I'd ever feel this way again. In fact, I almost forgot about . . . what I'd like to forget about.

Sunday, September 16

I went to Rock Port with Mom to get some real estate option papers signed. It was a long, boring day. Well . . . a lot of it was long and boring. The rest was nice. I like being with Mom. She's the only one I can be myself with. My real, real, real, real, real AIDS self with.

I've decided not to tell the gaggle about . . . it. In fact, I'm trying to pretend I don't even have . . . it. Missy said for me to go day by day and do what feels right.

Oh, Self, it's soooooooo painful to know that my blood is . . . DEADLY . . . that I could literally kill the people I love and want to protect the most just by being careless. I worry every minute that I'll be in an accident or something with someone whose life is more precious to me than my life itself . . . and that we'll both be bleeding and . . . they'll get even one drop. I wonder if anyone else in the world feels this much pain and responsibility. Missy tells me not to worry, but what kind of person would I be then? I worry so about Mom too. What if? What if?

1:02 P.M.

I woke up silently screaming. I didn't even know you could do that, but I did. Anyways, I dreamed that Mom had *it,* and I didn't, and she fell and cut herself on the glass she was holding. It was horrible . . . horrible . . . horrible. I wanted to help her, but the glass had shattered and cut me too. I can't bear to think about it, but I was afraid of her, deathly afraid. I wanted to run away! To run and keep running forever!!

I wonder if Mom ever feels that way about me. I'm sure she must! She must! Everybody must! But they don't know. They don't know, and I'm never going to let them. . . . Never. . . . Never. When I die, Mom can just say pneumonia did it, or something.

I've GOT TO DECIDE HOW TO TREAT LEW, WHAT TO TELL *HIM.* There are nine jillion ways I could do it. I could just drop him, pretending I'd met someone else in Arizona . . . or I could tell him the truth . . . or I could just act like nothing's happened . . . or I could just kill myself. No, Catholics don't do that. Besides, Mom would kill me if she knew I'd even thought about killing myself. How many times have I said that?

Monday, September 17

I saw Lew at school, and it's like absolutely nothing had happened in between. We sat on the grassy knoll and shared lunch, like the gaggle always does, and it was life as usual.

I had one scary little moment when Lew reached over and took a bite of my sandwich. I know Missy tells me people can't get *it* from stuff like that, but . . . I just wish I could wash away all the nagging little feelings. Do you think I ever will, Self? Please say yes.

Wednesday, September 19

Sorry I didn't talk with you yesterday, Self, but the gaggle was sooooo busy. We're starting on a class science project, and, of course, Lew is in charge, so his "little harem" had to go do as he commanded. It's going to be a most mag project! Right? Right! We're getting an early start for the School Science Fair in November then on to Region in January.

Friday, September 21

4:10 P.M.

. . . Confidentially, Self, it seems like I have to run to keep up with all the other kids who are only walking. I guess I'm just not getting enough rest. I'll sleep in Sunday, but tonight Jamie Leeds is having a party. Our gaggle is not too thrilled about going because most of those kids are into drugs, but . . . well, a dumb party is better than no party at all, right? Part of me wants to say *wrong,* but we, the gaggle, are straight and sober. I don't know about Dorie, though . . . she's acting kind of different . . . and she said she climbed out of her window and went "dusting" up Arch Canyon last Wednesday with Freddy. I really hope she's being careful . . . whatever the heck that means.

Saturday, September 22

12:59 P.M.

Jamie's party was pretty fun, at least for Lew and me. We sat out by the pool in the moonlight, and he told me all about his last few weeks. He lives such an exciting life. His big brothers are really good to him and his mom, and they have a gigantic extended family, cousins by the dozens and lots of uncles who are, to quote him, "fantastic father figures financially, socially, spiritually and family-wise." Then he hugged me and kissed me. Nice, warm, we-belong-together kisses. We committed that we wouldn't French-kiss after . . . you know, and I'm really glad, because "body fluids". . . . Oh, go away, go away, go away, you miserable spoil-everything thoughts.

Sunday, September 23

What a nice, slow, restful day. Mom and I slept in, then went out to the country club for a really, really mag brunch. Her company has a membership there, and I love it! It's like being part of the Rich and the Famous. I ate like a starving African and had three desserts. The dessert buffet table was so yummy I wanted one of each, but resisted because of the great discipline Lew and I have. See, the discipline thing is helping me in all areas of my life . . . I wish!!

Lew had to go to some little town south of here. One of his aunts had another baby, and they were going to name it today and have a big family do. I wish I could go with him sometime; it sounds like so much fun. Maybe when he's old enough to drive himself, he'll take me.

I can't believe it. Today Lew and I had lunch alone. It's the first day in forever when at least one of the gaggle hasn't been gaggling around. Anyways, he told me all about this new little cousin's blessing. He said he wishes I'd been there, and my heart almost leaped out of my throat and into his hands. He said he wanted us to be like his aunt Marcie and uncle Ted. Uncle Ted is a doctor, and he's so kind he even operates on and fixes up injured animals that the kids bring in. While they were there, Cody found a little bird that the cat had caught. Uncle Ted splinted its broken leg with a couple of toothpicks, and they made it a cage out of old wire.

Doesn't that sound like the nicest, kindest thing ever? I want Lew to be like Uncle Ted too, that kind, that caring, that everything. I tried to get him to tell me more about Aunt Marcie if I'm going to be like her, but the bell rang, and we had to go back to class. Later, I'll have to learn about my new idol.

Lew walked me home from the bus. It's one of the few, few afternoons when he doesn't have some kind of function or practice or job or something. I asked him to come in, but he wouldn't. I'm glad, because Mom wasn't home, and we've got forever ... well, he's got forever. I just ... you know ... maybe only YOU know.

Thursday, September 27

5:15 P.M.

It's Mom's birthday. She's got a date with nice Maury Marlow from her office. She and I will celebrate tomorrow.

10:41 P.M.

Tonight we went to an extra-credit concert. It was unexplainable. Lew and I sat and held hands and felt the music maybe even more than our ears heard it. There is something about classical music that's really different. Ordinarily I like *my* kind, but this was . . . sorry, no words.

Lew's brother Mike took us, and afterwards Lew walked me up to the lobby door, where he usually says good-bye, but tonight he took me all the way up to my apartment. In the hall by the elevator there's a little bench, and he sat me down and hugged me and kissed me till I felt like a fluttering something; then he reached in his pocket and pulled out the most beautiful, precious ring in the world and put it on my finger. "This is our till-we're-eighteen ring," he whispered, and I cried all over his shirt. I don't know when I have ever been so touched.

Can't write any more. I gotta go dream.

Sunday, January 6

11:11 A.M.

Dear Self:

It's been over three whole months you've been gone. How could you ever have lost yourself in that stack of old magazines? You almost got thrown away, you know. What would we ever have done then? Thank goodness Mom had me clean out the closet instead of Eleanore, who comes every two weeks. She'd have thrown you away for sure, as though you were totally useless. And that *you are not,* believe me!

I didn't get to write in you about Halloween,

Thanksgiving, Christmas or Dad's birthday, but they aren't much anymore anyway. I feel sorry for Dad and worry about him when I'm with Mom, and I feel sorry for Mom and worry about her when I'm with Dad. Divorce is hell on everybody. We try to buy our way out of our pain with presents and stuff, but it doesn't really work and the holiday spirit gets lost somewhere between the loneliness and the good past memories. Actually, I think holidays, when you're divorced (people never talk about it, but the kids are divorced too), may even be sadder than regular days. They certainly aren't like the festive, happy, together times they used to be. In fact, to tell the truth, something inside me sort of feels guilty when I get too giddy about the "good old times." I have to try to live in the *today, now, don't-look-back* period to keep from being depressed.

In a way it seems a shame to waste all those little-kid BD (before divorce) good memories, but trying to put up two Christmas trees with two single parents just isn't the same somehow. I wonder if I'd feel like this if I were still a little child playing with dolls and believing in Santa. I suspect so! But enough of examining my guts. Let's come out into the sunshine and the present. Or is the present pleasant? Oh, it is! It is! I'm feeling great and good and wonderful! Better, I think, than I've ever felt in my whole life. I have the energy to stay up with anybody in the whole world doing anything! Well, that's an exaggeration, but . . . you know.

I had to go to Dad's the day after Christmas. I didn't really *have* to, but I knew he wanted me to, and he has feelings. Mom and I clung together and cried when I left. Then I clung to Dad and cried when I had to come back.

I missed Mom like anything when I was at Dad's, but most of all, I missed the gaggle and guess who? Lew gave me a precious little gold heart pin for Christmas. In fact, he had Mom put it in my stocking to open Christmas morning because he and his mom went up to their uncle Ted's for Christmas. I gave him a "friendship ring," which I hope will be *more than that* in the future.

Dad tried hard to keep me entertained while I was there, but he kept having to run to the office for "a minute." I remembered, when I was little, asking him if it was going to be a lonnnnnnnnnnnng minute or a short minute, and at Christmastime I asked him that again. He grabbed me and slumped to the floor with me in his arms and hugged me like he was never going to let me go. I felt his tears on my face, and I'm sure he felt mine on his. I don't know why we were crying, because it was a most sacred, wonderful time. I didn't want to be separated from him again, ever ... ever ... ever! Together we relived each moment of my life ... well, almost each moment. All the good things anyway. He laughed about my almost having been born in the car before he and Mom could get to the hospital, and about how he was the hysterical, almost-out-of-control person that Mom had to soothe and comfort. In fact, he said she was so concerned about him that she wasn't even hardly aware of her contractions and kept trying to tell him jokes and stuff to calm him down. Then he told me about how, when I was lying in her arms in the hospital bed, we both looked like angels. I felt an ice chunk form in my belly. How could he ever have left her? I had a moment of wanting to reach over and pound him with my fists. Life is really complicated, isn't it?

Most of the time it was boring at Dad's, with no

friends, no gaggle, no Lew, no Mom. Boring . . . boring . . . boring, and I felt rotten . . . rotten . . . rotten.

When did I start feeling better? you ask. Well, I guess it came on slowly, I don't remember, I just realized one day that I wasn't tired all the time anymore. It's a very nice feeling, and I'm grateful. Once at Red's uncle's house we talked about "the sin of ingratitude," and after we'd gone to bed, Red and I whispered far into the night about that concept. About how being grateful draws you up and how being ungrateful drags you down. We both made a pact with spit on our fingers and our palms and everything about never, through the rest of our lives, being guilty of "the sin of ingratitude."

I'm glad I remember that. It was a nice memory. I have so, so, so much to be grateful for! I think I'll just lie here on the floor by the window and relive some of my blessings. Ummmm . . . I'll never forget when Dad and I got up before sunrise New Year's Eve day. We drove out to Superstition Mountain and watched the sun present itself in all its splendor. First the sky turned from black to gray to pink and gold. Then it was like the Disney movie *Fantasia,* with all the colors in eternity swirling around each other and us, to the background sounds of birds twittering and tweeting, leaves rustling, frogs croaking and our hearts madly pounding. It seemed like Dad and I were gods ourselves and had part in the panoramic creation of that spectacularly beautiful new day. I'm grateful for that one-of-a-kind experience. It helped me feel better about missing El's New Year's bash. I can see the gaggle now, playing crazy games and dancing and eating pizza and . . . I wish I could wish myself there right now. This very minute.

I'm grateful that I took Dad to the zoo for his

birthday too. We used to love to go to the zoo when I was little; especially we loved the monkeys. Dad said they still reminded him of *me*. After the zoo we went to Okay Jose's for lunch. I'd called him and told him we were coming, and he had lots of special gooey goodies for us. Jose is such a nice person, and it's a riot to go there. His one violin player is *really* funny. He tells silly jokes to music.

There's something else I would like to talk with you about, Self. Do other people feel like I do about birthdays? No one else's ever seems to be as nice and exciting as mine. Is it just because they're mine? Do other people feel the same way about theirs? Do you? Of course *you* do, 'cause you're *me!* Sometimes I almost forget that. So again, thank you, thank you. Thank *you* for being *you!*

Tuesday, January 22

I haven't stopped since I got home from Dad's. I miss him like everything, but my life is here, having fun, giggling with the gaggle and feeling, good, good, good, good. Except, I have to tell you about Dorie. She's been messing around with Fred Simmons, and now her period is late, she thinks. I don't know how she could be so careless, stupid, childish ... but I'm a fine one to talk. Anyway, she's facing some tough decisions, and the gaggle can't help her. She told us last week when we were having lunch on the knoll, and I think Lew took it probably harder than El or Red or me. We went over options! Tell her parents ... not tell her parents. Have an abortion ... not have an abortion. Marry Fred ... she said that was definitely out for him. Stay in school ... not stay in school. Keep the baby ... adopt the baby out.

The bell rang then, and I think we were all glad. This is too heavy . . . but at least she could share it, and it only hurts her, at least mainly. It's not contagious or life-threatening or . . . go away, thoughts.

The next day Lew and I took the city bus to the park. He said he needed to talk. I was soooooo scared. I thought maybe he was going to dump me just to be sure that . . . you know. But he didn't want to do that; he just wanted us to plan a support system for Dorie no matter what happened or what she decided to do. He's so mature. It's going to be a very lucky girl who gets him. I know it's not going to be me, *unless* there is a miracle in the medical field. Oh, I do believe in miracles . . . maybe . . . maybe . . . I hope . . . I hope!

Anyways—oops, anyway. Lew asked me not to say "anyways" anymore, and I'm trying to stop, but it's really hard. In fact, I didn't even know I said it. I guess it's just another one of my gruesome habits I've got to replace. Anyways . . . anyway, I forgot what I was going to say.

Lew says the most important thing in Dorie's life right now is for El and Red and me to be always there, always caring, especially if she truly is pregnant and she starts showing and kids make fun of her. Kids can be *so* mean, *so* heartless, *so* unempathetic. Is that a word? I guess only Lew would know for sure.

I've been so busy worrying about Dorie that I've hardly had time to worry about myself. Then today Officer Williams came over with two huge boxes full of yearbooks. Mom had told the police that I definitely would not go down there. *Anyway,* aren't you proud of me? That was such a bad habit to break. Anyway, he had yearbooks from every junior high in the nation that was named Abraham Lincoln Junior High. Officer Williams was very patient while I looked through them till my eyes crossed. He told me not to look for the name, because in all probability Throw-Up had used an alias. I couldn't believe that, but then, I couldn't believe any of the other stuff either.

At last, when I was about to give up, I found *his* picture—but he wasn't just barely eighteen like he'd said, he was *twenty-four-years old*. Gary Mitchem. He'd been a cute, innocent-looking kid back then in junior high. I wondered how he had ever gotten his life so mixed up and evil. How he could do something like he did to me, to a little kid.

Isn't it funny I always think of myself as a little kid when I think of Throw-Up, and all the rest of the time I want to feel grown up and able to take care of myself and want to be independent and not have Mom baby me and stuff. Now I want to have her hold me in her arms and rock me and sing lullaby songs to me and tell me all the things that are true aren't true.

Wednesday, January 23

12:07 A.M.

I've gotten so I can't sleep again. I see that cute blond curly-headed little junior-high-school kid, looking innocent and good and sweet, and I wonder, if I had ever been able to have a little boy, would he have looked like that, and then later grown up to be like . . . you know. It's a scary, scary thought that keeps going around and around in my head and won't go away. I wonder if I'd ever dare have children, even if

I ever could and I every would be here and all that. Maybe I could have that ... whatever test, and just have little girls. But then, if what happened to me happened to them, I couldn't stand that either. Oh, dear Self, do you ever notice how screwed up things seem in the middle of the night, or seem to make perfectly good sense when sometimes they don't make any sense at all?

3:06 A.M.

I remember how flattered I was when yuckety-yuck-yuck told me how pretty I was, and how soft I felt and how he loved to touch my baby skin, and how he called me baby skin. How all the time he told me how precious I was to him and how much he needed me and how he said I made him feel "not alone and lonely" and how I said he made me feel the same way, not alone and lonely too.

I don't know how I could ever have been so stupid, but I thought he was the most beautiful and brilliant human being who had ever lived and that he filled all the lonely, empty holes in my hole-filled life. Cheese Louise, how could I have been so sucked in, but I guess I'm not alone ... but I hope I am.

4:24 A.M.

I'm going to be a lively one at school tomorrow—I mean today. I've been thinking about a lecture we had one time in health and science. The guest psychologist was talking about how when you feel good in your head, you feel good in your body, and how we had to get things, and keep things, straight and honest and honorable in our lives. Oh, how I wish I'd done more than listen to her. She said too that too often kids would rather have a BAD FRIEND than no friend at all. That couldn't be true, because I've always had the gaggle since I was in grade school, but what about BOYFRIENDS? I'd never really had a boyfriend before *&=-+. And I should have been suspicious about him. When we were in the showers or had sleepovers, Dorie and El and Red all made fun of me because I looked like a boy when I didn't let my thick blond hair grow as long as it could. They could cut theirs short during the summers if they wanted to because they'd all shaped up literally. While me, the boys my age joked that you couldn't tell if I was coming or going because I was as flat in front as I was behind.

One day in the showers after gym, Dorie said my boobs looked like two fried eggs. That made me feel *real* sexy, right?

Thursday, January 24

6:45 A.M.

My trusty old alarm clock just started the "Good Morning" routine. Man, I hardly slept at all. Maybe a zesty shower will get me moving like the TV commercial.

7:45 A.M.

I've got 15 minutes till the bus.

RIGHT HERE IN WRITING, I'M MAKING A SOLMEN PROMISE THAT I WILL NEVER, EVER, EVER THINK OF *&=-+ AGAIN. I'M GOING TO ERASE THAT PART OF MY LIFE RIGHT OUT OF MY BRAIN. DELETE IT FROM MY COMPUTER, CUT IT OUT OF MY LIFE. I hereby

do solemnly promise with a blood oath. . . .
OHHHHH, THE PAIN. I CAN FORGIVE, BUT MY
BLOOD CANNOT.

I CAN'T GO TO SCHOOL. BUT I CAN'T STAY
HOME EITHER. THAT WOULD BE EVEN
WORSE. HE'S HERE. HE'S PART OF EVERY LIT-
TLE AND BIG THING AND MOLECULE AND
DUST PARTICLE IN THE APARTMENT. I'VE
GOTTA GET OUT OF HERE. I WISH I NEVER
HAD TO RETURN.

Thursday, January 31

4:30 P.M.

I told the gaggle I had an internal-combustion
headache mixed with PMS. I don't even know ex-
actly what that means, but they bought it and left me
alone. Thank goodness Lew is working on some
newspaper thing for the new sports program, so he's
just a "Hi" shadow in the hall these days. When am
I ever going to tell him? How can I tell him? Should
I tell him? I feel I'll explode if I don't, but I'll disin-
tegrate if I do. BUT YOU'RE NOT THINKING
ABOUT THAT ANYMORE, RETARD PERSON,
REMEMBER? THINK ABOUT THE BIG GAME
WITH SPRING VALLEY IN A COUPLE OF
WEEKS AND THE VALENTINE DANCE AFTER-
WARDS. OKAY, I WILL! I CAN! AND I AM!

Tuesday, February 5

5:54 P.M.

Guess who was waiting for me when I got home
from school? Officer Williams and my mom. They

both seemed so serious I thought something terrible had happened. I mean to Dad or someone. But it wasn't that, thank goodness. It was just that the police were putting out another APB or something, which I guess is like wanted posters or something, on *&=-+. They wanted me to search my memory and think if I had ever seen *&=-+ with any other kids. Of course I mentioned Margie. I was so depressed I couldn't even remember her last name till I looked it up in the yearbook. Then, thank goodness, Missy came and helped me relax so I could think straight again. After a while I dimly recalled the time when I'd seen *&=-+ with a couple of kids in his old beat-up convertible. Missy and the policeman had me lie down on the couch and close my eyes, and Missy softly rubbed my arms and hands as they tried to have me clear my mind of everything but the car and the kids. After a while I recalled that one of the girls had been in the junior high band runoffs at Charlesville last year. They had me remember her band, our colors, their colors—and I did! Ours were blue and gold, and theirs were green and white. Officer Williams was thrilled about that and said he could easily find out what junior high school in the area had green-and-white colors.

For a minute I relaxed, thinking this whole gig was over, and then he hit me with the fact that he'd be back in a few days with *that* yearbook, and I'd have to pick out the girl, maybe the other one too. I knew I couldn't pick out the second girl, but I was too tired and defeated to mention it.

6:30 P.M.

I am so exhausted ... WHEN IS THIS THING
EVER GOING TO END? ARE THEY EVER GO-
ING TO LET ME ALONE? HOW CAN I EVER
GET MY LIFE SORTED OUT WHEN I'M SO IN-
VOLVED IN EVERYBODY ELSE'S? I FEEL TER-
RIBLE.

Wednesday, February 6

2:15 A.M.

Dear Self:

I just woke up from one nightmare to find myself
in a real one. I had recalled one day when Dorie and
El and I were riding our bikes down by Luke Clear
Lake, and I saw out of the corner of my eye *&=-+
and a little boy, maybe even in grade school, going
down the path toward the unfinished end. I remember
wishing all the chiggers and no-see-ums and mosquitoes in the world would get him; then I pushed it out
of my mind and yelled that I'd race the kids to the
end of the trail. Now my brain is racing a katrillion
miles an hour ... surely he wouldn't with a little boy
maybe seven or eight? I had no way in the world to
identify that kid—I just saw his back. If he did ...
would he have it too?

Oh, horrors, horrors, horrors, I think I'll wake up
Mom and tell her; then she can tell Officer Williams.
I can't possibly stand any more and besides, I think
I've got a fever. I think I'll go hop in bed with Mom
and just cuddle and let all the pain and anguish be
warmed and loved away. But maybe I shouldn't ...
it's my period and Missy said body fluids, especially
blood and semen ... oh, how I wish I knew more.

105

I've got to get some books. I wouldn't give *this* to anyone . . . anyone in the world, especially my sweet, wonderful mom.

3:10 A.M.

I really am sick. I want to call Mom, but I don't want to. She's had enough heartaches with me . . . but I've got to . . . I'm scared. Maybe I should just lie still and die. I wonder if this is how it happens. I hope it doesn't hurt this much when it happens to Margie and the two girls and the little boy, if they all have it too.

4:14 A.M.

Oh, dear Self:
It's 4:14, and I'm not dead yet . . . but I can't stand it anymore. My chests hurts so much, and I can't breathe . . . why don't I die. Oh, Mom, Mom, Mom, come help me. I cried her name out loud, and I'm trying not to. Help me, Mom . . . help me, somebody. Please, please help me die, but don't let me die alone.

Saturday, February 9

9:32 A.M.—Hospital

Dear Self:
I'm so glad Mom brought me a new loose-leaf. I wouldn't want her to read my old one. I keep it hidden under my shoebox in the closet. She doesn't need to know all my sorrows and fears. She's got enough of her own with me and Dad, and her job and everything! Poor Mom. Poor, poor Mom.

She even broke up with Maury, her nice friend from the office, after she found out I had . . .

I've been in the hospital for I don't know how many days with pneumocystis carinii pneumonia (also known as pneumocystis pneumonia, or PCP); that's what it says in this little book my new doctor gave me. Dr. Talbert said he couldn't treat me anymore because of my . . . it's not his field. I guess I might as well face it and use the word *HIV*.

HIV

HIV

WHICH LEADS TO AIDS

AIDS

AIDS

WHICH LEADS TO . . . . . .

Now I'm being morbid and paranoid and dumb.

Dr. Sheranian seems kind and caring, but I notice that he's always very sterile with gloves and stuff. The nurses are the same. Dr. Talbert and his nurses always were just like people . . . that's dumb, because these people are people, but they're kind of aliens too, white aliens, sometimes green, but I guess that's just the hospital rules. I WANT OUTTA HERE. NOW! NOW! NOW! BUT WHO CARES WHAT I WANT!

11:59 A.M.

More tests, more medications, more IV stuff. My chest hurts, my neck hurts, my bum hurts. I hurt every inch of my body like I didn't know hurt could hurt! I can hardly read my writing, but I can't stop. It's like the one string that holds me here. Wherever here is. I guess the meds are kicking in, because I feel myself floating off into lala land. The hurts still hurt, but

it's

sooo

o

o

f

a r

a

w

a

y

Tuesday, February 12

8:02 A.M.

I asked the nurse what day it was, and she said Tuesday. I don't have a clue how long I've been here, but it seems forever. Anyway, I'm feeling better.

Better than what?

A lot better than how I've felt for some time, so there!

Self, I'm glad I've got you to talk to, otherwise I'd know for sure *it* was affecting my mind. Mom promised she'd tell the gaggle I'd gone to Dad's again. I hate to ask her to lie . . . but . . . you know how it is.

2:07 P.M.

I know I'm getting better because my handwriting is almost readable. It's funny how weak I am, though. Even the pencil seems heavy.

I've gotta leave you now because I'm going to start reading up on some of the stuff Dr. Sheranian left. He smuggled me in a piece of See's candy, which I said was the only thing in the world I wanted to eat. He said if I told anyone about it, he'd make me clean all the bedpans on the floor for two weeks, and if I gave him any more trouble after that, he'd make me do all the BM pans in the whole hospital *forever!*

I called him a hard-nose, and we laughed. It's the first time I've felt capable of laughing in a longgggggg time. Two nurses came in then, and he told them to "get their butts out," that we were having a deep medical conference.

5:30 P.M.

Mom just left. She had an appointment to show an apartment house, and I know we must really NEED money now. I'm going to start seriously reading and take notes so I'll know what the heck I really have and how it works. Missy tried to tell me a little, but like I said, I always had the feeling that she was trying to shield me as she prepared me for whatever. We'll see.

Thursday, February 14

7:30 P.M.

Valentine's Day—what a bummer! I'm reading a brochure, *Teenagers and AIDS*. It's scary! I thought I was almost the only one who had it at first, outside of the big cities, where people have indiscriminate sex and use IVs and stuff. The book says that about 30 percent of people who have AIDS are diagnosed in their twenties, WOW! that means most were infected in their teens. It also says that AIDS is spreading faster and faster among kids, who don't even dream it could happen to them, and that they are the most at-risk of all people!

I didn't even understand what AIDS (Acquired Immune Deficiency Syndrome) meant before. It always seemed so dull and boring and sterile when it was talked about at school. Believe me, it's not dull now. I can't learn enough.

Okay, "Acquired" means it's a disease that you can be infected with—that you *get!* It's not an illness people are born with, like hemophilia or something.

"Immune Deficiency" means a breakdown in your body's defense system against disease. AIDS is a tiny germ or a virus that can live inside a living cell.

The AIDS virus is called HIV, which means human immunodeficiency virus. It works like this: When the HIV virus enters your body, it invades a cell that is part of your immune system. That cell turns into a major virus *factory,* churning out copies of the HIV invader. Those copies of the original virus attack other cells in your body that are the key parts of your immune system. Then you start getting every kind of disease that you are exposed to, including rare ones that you would never get with a good healthy immune system and normal health.

When people have normal health, their immune system can defeat most kinds of viruses, including those that cause flu. But when you have AIDS, your body won't fight off infection hardly at all. Actually, over time you become less and less able to fight off any and every disease.

EVENTUALLY ANY ILLNESS YOU'RE SUSCEPTIBLE TO CAN LEAD TO YOUR DEATH.

Now it's not *your* death, it's my death! And I don't like it!

I DO NOT WANT TO DIE! I'M JUST FIFTEEN YEARS OLD! THIS IS SUPPOSED TO BE THE BEST PART OF MY LIFE. WHEN I TURN FROM A GIRL INTO A WOMAN! WHEN LEW AND I ... WHICH WE NEVER WILL ... Oh, dear God, how can I ever stand it?

Friday, February 15

2:30 A.M.

I'm writing by the little spark from my Bunny Night Light clock, which I've had since I was five years old, remember? Mom can't understand how it has existed through our many moves and changes. The thing I can't understand is how my eyes can adjust like a cat's to see in the almost dark.

Anyway, I've been thinking about me and all the things I'll never be able to do.

Most of all, I'm feeling very hollow inside about Lew and me. We'll never be able to "MAKE LOVE." I don't mean that animalistic, almost cannibalism kind that El and I saw that time on her uncle's TV X-rated channel, which we watched while were baby-sitting. It was crude, rude, filthy, degrading and disgusting ... like ... you know.

I don't want it to be that way. I want it to be like the way I feel inside sometimes, soft and warm and belonging with a glowing, tingling building up inside until it just takes over completely. Me and Red talked about how we thought it would feel, one time when I was sleeping over at her house. Now I'll never really know. Well, maybe I'll know ... but what if ...

I couldn't stand it if I gave it to Lew. I could never, never, never forgive myself for that through the eons of eternities.

I'm going to read everything that has ever been written about the HIV virus and full-blown AIDS. I guess I really did think that just drug users and bar-hopping gay guys on the streets of San Francisco got it; that's mostly all you see on the news. No, not really . . . that's what I wanted to believe, I guess. But at least in a few weeks I will know every single thing! I'm sure Dr. Sheranian will help me. He's a specialist in the field.

9:10 A.M.

This morning when Dr. Sheranian made his rounds, he asked the two interns, or whoever they were, to go on so he could talk to me. I really feel a lot better. I asked him how I could give AIDS to someone like my mother, or someone—I didn't say a boyfriend, but I know he knew from the way he patted my cheek and ran his fingers through my hair.

He told me no one need ever catch it from me if I'm careful, and he turned to page 23 of one of my leaflets and told me to read that part. Then the nurse came in to do her thing. Gotta go and let her prod me and poke me and put more stuff in my IV and give me more pills, etc. BUT I BELIEVE DR. S., AND *I AM NOT GOING TO WORRY ANYMORE!*

9:57 A.M.

I lied! I am going to worry some more! I am going to worry every minute of every hour for the rest of my life!!!

NO, I just wanted it to be easy, and I've got to be realistic . . . it's not going to be!

Oh, dear God, how could this have happened to me? Please, God, don't let it ever happen to any other girl like me. Please, please, please don't. What could I ever have done to deserve this?

My tears are like gagged pieces of ice cutting up my eyeballs and hamburgering my face. That means blood . . . and my blood is poison . . . I'm afraid to even touch it myself.

Oh, please, I hope I die soon.

12:06 P.M.

My fever has popped way up again. It's so depressing, because I thought I was going home tomorrow. Dr. S. came by and said it's because I've let myself get so riled up. He's talked me back down to reality and sanity, and he's going to bring me a positive book about people with AIDS. Dr. S. says that's the kind of attitude I've got to teach myself to have. Dr. S. always makes me feel better because he's not afraid to hug me and he laughingly tells me I'm a Paranoid Puddle afraid of my shadow. I said, "I'm like the lepers in the olden Bible days," and he gave me a nogie and said leprosy is now called Hansen's disease and can be cleared up easily with antibiotics, which hopefully they'll be able to do soon with AIDS.

They've given me something and I'm getting sleepy.

I'm so glad he came. I guess AIDS isn't the boogey-boo I let myself believe it was. I am a Scaredy Cat Paranoid Puddle . . . I mean . . . I was. Past tense.

Saturday, February 16

11:29 A.M.

Dr. S. had a nurse bring the book he talked about up to me. It's about people who were *so* brave, and *so* positive, and treated *so* badly. Yet they didn't whine and cry-baby like I do. I'm so glad I get to see AIDS from their side. I can't stop reading.

?Whatever Day It Is?

7:32 A.M.

Yippie. Dr. S. came by and said I can go home. Mom will be picking me up in an hour or two or three or whatever wonderful time she gets here. I've been reading Dr. S.'s book almost steadily. The people in it are beginning to seem like wonderful, close, hurting friends. I wish I could have talked to them. More than that, I wish I could talk to *someone my own age!* Now!

It's killing me to keep all the heavy, growing, absorbing, taking-over-my-life stuff inside. But AIDS *isn't unbearable!* One guy, after he moved to his new town, had lots of friends, and everybody loved him, and they weren't scared or pulling away or anything. It's going to be like that for me too. It truly is, and I am sooo happy to know that. I've known it all along, actually. I was just doing my thing of being a boob.

I am going to be happy, happy, happy! AIDS is *not* casually contagious! No one will be afraid of me. I'm going to tell everybody as soon as I get out of here. It will be such a relief, and it will be just like always.

8:22 A.M.

The bubble has burst again! My world has changed from a sphere of sunshine to one of black, depressing, sucking-down jello.

I was standing in my doorway waiting for Mom to come, and two people dressed like astronauts went into the room next to mine. I couldn't imagine why they had hats and body suits and stuff on. Then I heard someone say an AIDS patient had just died there. That cracked me into little pieces.

If AIDS is not as contagious as they say, then how come all that's necessary? BODY FLUIDS? Oh, yes, it's got to be BODY FLUIDS, but what in the hell all over does *that* mean?

8:43 A.M.

Maybe they are careful like that with all really contagious diseases, do you think? Maybe! I'LL WORRY ABOUT THAT TOMORROW ... AFTER I TALK TO DR. S. But I'm not going to see him again. I'm never going to see him again!

Tuesday, February 19

6 A.M.

It's so wonderful to be home, and loved and feeling well again. The sliding-glass door to the terrace is open, and Imperical is singing his little heart out in his cage. The sun is coming up outside and inside my heart as well. I want to dance and sing that old song that my grandma liked:

*"Whoop a dee dee, I'm glad I'm me. There's no
one else I'd rather be. I smile on every flower
and tree. Whoop a dee dee, I'm glad I'm me!"*

I'm sitting here reading the twelve letters that the
gaggle wrote to me, over and over. They love me so
much. I'm a fortunate person to have friends like
that. I'm going to have Mom call them tonight and
tell them I'm back.

I wonder if she'll let me go back to school tomorrow. Probably not, but I'm sure I can go Thursday or
Friday.

I'm still feeling a little weak, but the *old ME* is
back, ravenous and raring to go! Go! Go! Go! Go!

I wonder who will come to see me first. I hope it's
guess who. I can't wait to see his beautiful, warm,
world-embracing smile and feel his soft, sometimes
not so soft hand, after he's been working after school
and playing whatever sport is on and everything. I
hope he'll hug me right in front of Mom . . . but I
know he won't! El and Red and Dorie will, though
. . . but I want *his* hug. I need it. I honest, truly do.
It would be the most healing thing there is.

Wednesday, February 20

6:17 P.M.

Dorie and El and Red came over right after school.
Since I saw them, it seems like a forever of forevers.
We talked about everything and everyone as though
I'd been away for years. Yet it was still like I'd seen
them just yesterday.

Everything is grand and glorious and exciting with
everything and everybody except . . . Dorie still

hasn't had her period. That's scary. She's used those little packages that come out pink if you are . . . and it's pink or vice versa. We were all so upset about her that no one really thought much about me, and that was wonderful for a change. I'm really glad I'm not her! I don't know what I'd do either. She says she decides one thing one day and then changes her mind the next. . . . It's a horrible decision either way, and she's only got weeks to decide if she's going to have an abortion. That would be soooo hard . . . imagine the little tiny baby being sucked out kicking and screaming and thrown away. I wonder what they do with all those dead babies.

Oh, now I'm being dumb. Abortion isn't anything now . . . or is it? Oh, cheese. I'm so glad I'm not her. But if the baby were mine and Lew's, I would never, never, never give it up. He wouldn't want me to, I know. *He* wouldn't let me. But what would I do? I'm just fifteen years old. Who would tend the baby? Would I have to live with my mother forever? Would I have to quit school? No wonder Dorie looks so tired and scared. What a *horrific* decision! I heard Mom use that word and loved it. I wondered when I'd ever use it. I certainly didn't think it would be about anything this HORRIFIC. Not that babies are horrific— but, well, they're not what you think.

Once Mom's sister, Aunt Milly, brought her baby over for us to tend while she and Uncle Charles went on a vacation for a long weekend. I looked forward to it so much I couldn't sleep before. Then after Baby Bonny came, I couldn't sleep because it seemed like she cried all night and because of her wetting and crying and pooping and throwing up and needing her bottle, and wanting to be rocked and walked and bathed and dressed and changed and changed and changed!! I found that babies are not like kittens that you can feed and water once a day and play with when you want to. *They* write the rules! Another thing, you wouldn't think that a pretty, darling little creature like a baby could smell so bad or get poop up to their armpits . . . ukkie . . . it was gross—and so often!

Before then, I sometimes felt if I had a baby it would give me something of my very own to love and to be JUST MINE. That if I had a baby, the two of us would start a whole new world. When Merry Beth, our sixteen-year-old neighbor, had her baby and decided to keep it, I remember I almost envied her. Someone to be with *all* the time, to love, to have her love me and be dependent upon me. Secretly, Self, I now know I don't want that much dependence . . . at least not now . . . maybe someday when we're more mature, huh?

Tuesday, February 26

5:59 P.M.

I'm sooooo depressed. Dorie, my very dearest and kindest-hearted friend, just left. I'm so glad she had *me* to talk to and that Mom wasn't here. I shouldn't say talk to . . . I should say talk *at,* because I certainly didn't have any profound answers.

I can't believe that Fred dumped her. How could that be? How in this world, or any other world, could a boy just dump a girl he'd made pregnant? I wonder if the stupid jackass thought she'd done it by herself.

Imagine him meeting her at the bottom of the gym steps and, just out of the blue, telling her he didn't think they should see each other anymore. Her pregnant and him just acting like it was nothing and all her fault and responsibility and like that.

I think I'd have ripped his heart out through his eyeballs, or at least screamed and hollered so everyone in creation could have heard me and at least know what a lousy, uncaring, selfish, rotten, miserable, sleaze maggot he was. AND . . . to make it even worse . . . when she started crying, he asked her how he'd ever know it was his anyway . . . and it was *her* responsibility to take care of those things.

I'm sooooo sad. I wish there was something I could do. I walked her to the bus stop, but I'm helpless . . . everybody is helpless. She just has to choose between horrific and more horrific.

Thursday, February 28

7 P.M.

Dorie's mom let her come over after school to study and have dinner. LET HER? Here *she's* about to become a mother, and she has to ask *her* mother if she can come study. I keep thinking of her dragging that little baby around with her every minute of the night and day, but I don't know how she can ever, ever give it up either. What if someone adopted it who abused it? Oh, the poor little kid. And if she'd had an abortion, then . . . I think I'm worrying about it almost as much as she is. I'm so glad she's got me. El and Red are still their old happy-go-lucky, light-minded selves, and me and Dorie are . . . Sometimes I want to confide in her about my problem so much, it's like a real hurting, aching, twisting pain inside me, but I can't. She has enough problems of her own right now.

Saturday, March 2

7 A.M.

Dorie's going to sleep over, and tomorrow Mom's going to take us to what we call Buttercup Lake. I'm so glad. Both of us need to go lie in a bright meadow and listen to the sounds of happiness and almost spring, with the lake's waves flopping softly on the sandy beach in the background. Mom's taking a big lunch, but we'll stop at the Squirrel Corners Diner on the way back. Mom says both of us are always running on *EMPTY*.

I finally got up the nerve to ask Dorie last night if she wasn't even using birth control pills when ... She said she was, but that sometimes she forgot. At first I was mad at her and wanted to give her RE-SPONSIBILITY LECTURE 997 that Ms. Marsden, our health teacher, gives us every so often, but I couldn't. Who am I to lecture her on being responsible daily for taking the pill, when Mom has to nag at me half the time about feeding my bird? Besides, Dorie said Fred used a condom—well, most of the time he did ... but they're *expensive*. Dorie said they cost about $6.00 a dozen. That would be ... but I don't want to think about it. I won't think about it. I won't let myself think anything but Buttercup Lake and big fat curly French fries at Squirrel Corners.

Monday, March 4

5:30 A.M.

I woke up really early this morning and just relived the weekend. It was so wonderful and quiet and beautiful and fantasy-world-escaping. Dorie and

120

Mom and I chased each other through barely yellow meadows of budding buttercups. We pretended they were each a sunshine pocket about ready to open. We laughed and teased and sat on a log. Mom brought her guitar, which she hasn't played in forever, and we sang all the songs she knew. Then Dorie and I taught her the new ones we know. It was glorious, it was heavenly. I wish every day of the rest of my life could be just like it.

Tuesday, March 5

4:59 P.M.

Lew and I took our sandwiches and ate as we walked down by the old firehouse. We sat on the lawn there and talked about how longgggg since we've really had any alone time together. He hugged me, and it healed every molecule in my body and brain and soul. We moved over behind the giant shrubs on the side, and he kissed me. It was like sparklers and Christmas and the Fourth of July and blessed Easter all mixed together.

I hate to admit it, but I really wanted to ... you know ... but I didn't, too. I know we shouldn't and all that, but sex is such a powerful force! I've wanted to ask Dorie about all the details of it. It was so ... gaggy and dirty ... with *&=-+, but I can feel it will be beautiful and wholesome with Lew when he's ready. I know it's funny, at least I think it is, for the boy to be more hold-backish than the girl, but then maybe it isn't, too. Boys think about their futures and their responsibilities and trade-offs in life just like we do, or at least they should! And Lew does! Thank goodness he does! I don't think I would ever feel this way about another boy in the whole world . . . or would I?

I dimly remember one of the *"mother's lectures on sex"* Mom tried to give and I tried not to listen to. She said that sex could be the greatest force in life after self-preservation, and that often it became even greater than self-preservation, like in war times when men would go into almost sure-death situations for a woman, and times when people just get carried away with their emotions, and their hormone output becomes greater than their brain input. I hope that never happens with me. Do you think it ever could, Self? Especially now when I might give . . . you know . . . oh, forget the whole thing. Sex causes more trouble than it's worth, I think!!!!

See ya, I gotta go start dinner. Mom's bringing home a lady from the office so they can work on a project afterwards.

Thursday, March 7

Dear Self:

I haven't written for a couple of days because somehow you got put somewhere . . . and . . . well . . . I'm so disorganized. Besides, I've been trying not to think much, I've been feeling so rotten. Dr. S. says that lots of people who are HIV positive feel pretty good for five or six or even seven years, but because of my low immune system to begin with, I've got an infection in my eyes that just doesn't seem to want to clear up.

3:30 P.M.

Mom took me out of school early to see Dr. S., rather the eye guy he had me go see. Another kick in the heart and head. How many more can I take? One medicine I can take will save my eyesight; another will keep me alive, but I can't take both. I can take AZT, which is a medicine that slows the AIDS virus, or I can take Ganciclovir, a medicine that can stop this blinding eye infection. But since both drugs cause anmeia, most people can't tolerate them together.

Wow, what a choice! GO OFF AZT, WHICH KEEPS PEOPLE SYMPTOMLESS LONGER, OR STAY ON AZT AND GO BLIND. DECISION TIME. CELEBRATION TIME, RIGHT?

The goofy, mutant-looking doctor, who even has a science fiction accent, LOOKED AT ME LIKE I was a straggly little mongrel puppy that had just been run over, and told me I had a third choice. I started to laugh and cry at the same time, I was so confused. After a while Mom got me calmed down a little, and Dr. Mutant was able to tell us that researchers had developed a new way of delivering the eye medicine so it won't cause anemia. They implant minuscule sustained-release pellets inside the eyeball. Now doesn't that sound fun?

This keeps the drug out of the bloodstream and keeps it inside the eyeball, where it is needed. It's released in a steady, slow rate, which means you don't have the ups and downs of daily infusions. I don't think I could stand that "daily" bit.

Dr. Goofy Mutant gave me a copy of an article

about Ganciclovir and about a dozen other new approaches being developed to control what they call "opportunistic infections." They are the usually harmless germs that attack people with AIDS-weakened immune defenses.

Lucky, lucky me, I get to be a guinea pig for some of the pharmaceutical industry's more than 40 new drugs that are being tested against the viruses, bacteria and other microscopic invaders common among the *UNCHOSEN* FEW OF US.

"Of all the AIDS-related illnesses, cytomegalovirus—CMV—retinitis is among the most frequent and devastating." Dr. M. says it strikes about 20 percent of AIDS patients. Unless treated, it means certain loss of sight. I couldn't handle that. I couldn't write to you, dear Self. I couldn't see flowers or trees or sunshine . . . or my friends . . . or LEW. I couldn't, I positively couldn't, stand not seeing LEW.

I've got to choose between Ganciclovir and a newer medicine called Foscarnet by tomorrow. What a choice. Ganciclovir causes anemia and Foscarnet harms the kidneys.

Given the old-fashioned way, both drugs require daily intravenous infusions, taking two or three hours to complete. Patients must have catheters permanently implanted to receive the infusions. And if that weren't enough, the virus typically returns after two months of treatment, requiring still higher doses.

I think I'll opt for cutting open my eye and putting in the pellets. That will last for six months, and a year-long type will be tested soon. We'll see.

Happy dreams to you—I don't know about me.

Tuesday, March 19

Dear Self:
I'm glad we're together. I need you. I really do. It's amazing how I trust Mom, and my friends and Lew. I *really* trust Lew. But there's still so much of me that I can't even trust with him. But I've got to. Soon I will tell them all about me. Life is soooooo unfair. I wish I knew how to do it.

Friday, March 22

Dear Self:
Sorry I missed writing in you Wednesday and Thursday. What kind of friend am I, even to you? Myself?
Anyway, at school today a couple of kids were teasing Dorie because she's beginning to show. I felt so bad for her I wanted to punch them into their lockers and throw away the combinations.

Saturday, March 23

10 P.M.

It's been such a fun day. Mom took the old gaggle to Wildwood, except Lew, who had to work as usual. We rode on the crazy, upchucking rides and chased each other with water guns. We were like little kids again, noisy and silly, loud and dumb. I wonder if there will ever be another day like this. El got sick and almost threw up on the Whirl-a-Wheelie; Red slipped in a mud puddle and had to go all day with the seat of her white shorts stained brown. I spilled catsup and mustard from my hot dog all down the front of my shirt, and Dorie got hit in the nose with a ball. It was like the old days when we were young and life was sweet and our problems were simple.

I DON'T WANT TO GROW UP!
I WANT TO GO BACKWARDS!

Monday, March 25

3:29 P.M.

I've been sick again. Dr. S. says my HIV is progressing soooo much faster because of my lowered immune system. This time it's a stupid kidney infection.

Why couldn't I be like other people who have five or ten or so years before they even know they have it? What I wouldn't give for five or ten or so more good years.

Actually, Dr. S. doesn't even call it HIV anymore; he calls it AIDS. I don't know when he started that. I guess, like usual, I just didn't want to listen.

I wonder how many good years I really do have.

Maybe it's time I should start doing some serious thinking about dying. I wonder what dying is like. Will it hurt? Where will I go? Is there really a Heaven, or will the particles from my body just join with the other particles of the earth for topsoil or dust bunnies or something else totally useless? I don't want that! I WON'T BELIEVE THAT! *THERE IS A HEAVEN . . . AND A GOD!* AND IT'S WHITE AND CLEAN AND PURE, AND GOD IS CREATING OTHER WORLDS, AND I WILL BE A HELPER IN SOME WAY. AND I'LL GO ON AND ON THROUGH FOREVERS OF ETERNITIES . . . BE-

ING ME ... DOING WONDERFUL, CONSTRUC-
TIVE, HAPPY AND FULFILLING THINGS.

In time, Lew and Mom and Dad and all the other
people I love will come up to Heaven too, and we'll
have a wonderful and grand and glorious reunion
with Great-Grandma and Grandpa Ivy and all my
pets that died: Catsup, Red Dog and Fluffer, and ...
but what if I go to Hell? I don't think I've been that
bad ... I haven't been that good either ... I guess I
better start saying a few Hail Marys and Our Fathers
just in case.

Tuesday, March 26

Dear Self:
Sometimes I'm such a goof-goon-type person. For
a while I'll feel like a leper from Bible times; then
I'll be the old me, happy and witty and show-offish.
Sometimes I'm conforming, then not conforming;
and up, then down; me, then *YOU!* Wow! I think *it's*
gone to my brain.

Wednesday, March 27

11:12 P.M.

Today everything started out at the top of the lad-
der. We had short classes so we could take the bus to
Lakewood to watch Lew's tennis team. He was mag
... magnif ... and magnificent!!! El and Dorie and
Red and me screamed till we were all hoarse. We
beat the Lake Lizards hands down. Then we all went
to El's for junk food, as though we hadn't consumed
enough during the game. Nick and Mandy came too,
and Barney and Freddie Fields and a couple of team
guys. We laughed till we cried as we went over all

the game moves, both dumb and brilliant. Lew held my hand a lot of the time, and I was in heaven.

Lew's brother Mike, who was supposed to pick Dorie and Red and Lew and me up from our school, was late; so after the others had all gone, we sat out on the front steps and counted stars and waited for him. I don't know what happened, but after a while I just couldn't hold it in anymore, and I told them about my having AIDS. It was hard to get the word out at first; then the whole thing flooded all over. It was a great relief, for in some scary way I expected them all to pull away. They didn't, though. After a stunned moment, they were all on top of me, till I felt like I was at the bottom of a football pileup.

Thank goodness we've had a lot of good educational stuff at school about AIDS, so they weren't afraid of me and stuff like I guess, deep inside, I'd somehow thought they would be.

We all cried together, and Lew kept holding my hand tighter and tighter and repeating over and over, "Why you? . . . Why you? . . . Why you?"

I didn't tell them then *how* I got it, and I guess they all believed I got it from blood at one of my hospital visits. Maybe someday I'll tell them that too . . . but maybe I won't.

It's such a relief. So much so that when I got home I had to wake Mom up and tell her. She pulled me down into her bed, and we snuggled for a while before I came in to write in you.

Aren't you relieved, Self? Isn't it grand?

4:53 P.M.

Today I cut my finger on my locker and had to go to the school nurse for a Band-Aid. I'd immediately wrapped my finger in a Kleenex and then put the Kleenex in a plastic bag I had in my purse, like Dr. S. had told me to do. It was important to be careful.

I wasn't prepared for the look on Mrs. Maggleby's face when I told her I had AIDS. She didn't noticeably pull back, but I saw a strange look snap on and off her face, like I'd seen once on a little kid in the playground when a big kid had hit him and he didn't know whether to run and hide in his mom's protective skirts or to stay and fight. It was over in a second, and she again became the knowledgeable, in-control person who often talked to us about AIDS and herpes 2 and hepatitis B and all the other things we should be aware of.

It was a great relief when she asked me if I'd like to stay and talk, and she offered to write me an excuse if I did.

It was nice to have someone to dump on, and she said she'd always be there for me, no matter what.

In a way, I'm glad it's over. It's hard work to keep a secret. She has to report it to the principal, but not to worry, this is an enlightened school.

Friday, March 29

5:16 P.M.

Good Friday? The worst Friday ever!

Enlightened school? Apparently during first class, the word leaked out about me, because by second class everyone was looking at me like I was from another galaxy, or like the stick-figure, big-headed Mars person in cartoons. I knew they knew! I could read it all over them. Even Mr. Lindstrom in my English class looked at me quickly, then looked away, like he didn't know how to act.

I tried to concentrate on Chapter 12, but my mind was jumping around like a frog inside my head. I guess if I was Marxie Koffer, who sat next to me, and she was me, I'd be curious and uncomfortable or something too. We've never had anyone in our school with AIDS before, that anyone knew about. Marxie smiled at me self-consciously, then buried her head in her book like a snake going down its hole. But the book couldn't hide her. She still had to look up at me once in a while to be sure . . . whatever.

It didn't get better. In the halls, the kids were all ganged up in little groups whispering wildly, and when I came by, everybody quieted down and tried to become invisible or tried to be too overly friendly. It was weird for all of us.

I tried not to get too weirded out, because I'm sure in their place I'd have done the same and felt the same . . . maybe just plain uncomfortable with something totally new and off the wall.

The gaggle and I had lunch together on the hill, and they all offered to defend me, but it wasn't defense I needed, it was . . . I guess just time. Everyone knows I'm not Typhoid Mary or anything . . . but I still noticed that when I went to the girls' room, no one wanted to use the stall after me. They all waited for one of the others. I could see it in the mirror as I washed my hands.

I keep telling myself to give them time . . . time . . . time. But I don't know how much time I've got.

Oh, that's morbid and dumb. But those dumb thoughts occasionally flash into my brain.

Wednesday, April 3

10:31 A.M. and Four Seconds

Things are about back to normal at school. Mrs. Maggleby, the school nurse, gave out little booklets again to everybody about AIDS, and I think that made us all feel better. In fact, some of the kids who were just cardboard cartoons before have gone out of their way to be nice. I'm glad I told. It's soooo much pressure off me.

Things aren't today like they were when Ryan White was in school in the 1980s. His family even had to move to another town because the people at his school wouldn't let their kids come to school if he was there. Isn't that about the saddest?

Thursday, April 4

10:10 A.M.—World History

We had the Wowest assembly. Mr. Chen, our science teacher's cousin, is touring America with an acrobat group. Two of the guys came and did things that all of us would have considered impossible. Then Mr. Chen explained how important concentration and mind control are to body control. It made us all want to work a little harder in school.

Sunday, April 7

11:04 P.M.

I'd like to tell you all the mag things that happened today out at Lew's uncle Morton's, but I'm just too tired ... and besides, I want to relive every fraction of a second of it over again and again and again in my dreams.

Monday, April 8

4:46 P.M.

Dear Self:
My periods are a big pain now. I can flush the tampons down the toilet, but I feel guilt because signs in each bathroom at school say not to. One day I tried to put the used one in a plastic bag in my purse, but ... I WILL NOT DO THAT AGAIN ... EVER. That is too degrading and humiliating—and what if I dropped my purse and it fell out? I'd die right there on the spot. I truly would; at least I hope I would.

Tuesday, April 9

Math Class

Our big MATH STATE REPORTS came back today, and I'm sooooo pleased. I got A-. If I hadn't been out of school so much, I'd have gotten an A, I'm sure. Lew and I decided at the beginning of the term that we would do our very best. I'm sure he got an A, but I won't know till tomorrow because he left early to practice something or other. Maybe I'll call him at home. I guess that's a good enough reason, don't you think?

Wednesday, April 10

7:30 P.M.

I should have known it was too good to last. Kids are mean and cruel and sadistic and evil and twisted. It was like the most nightmarish of all nightmares. I was just walking down the hall, minding my own business, when the twins, Mick and Mack, and Gregg turned the corner. The twins were tussling with Gregg, and when they saw me they started forcing him in my direction, giggling. "Give him a deep French kiss, Nancy. Give him a deep, wiggling French kiss"—they broke up with laughter—"and your special something as well." They were pressing him against my body, which was against my locker, and his forehead banged mine. I tried to yell, "Ouch," "HELP," but nothing came out. Other kids were walking down the hall, but it seemed hours before they pulled the three creatures from Hell off me.

The principal called Mom and she was there in minutes to rescue me. I don't think I'll ever go back to real school again. Home school wasn't so bad.

Thursday, April 11

2:45 A.M.

Principal Paula O'Raynie just left our house. She's pretty good at sweet-talking. Between her and Miss Shephard, the school counselor, I guess I accept that the boys were just being thoughtless, playful and dumb, and that I have to rise above their childish-

133

ness, but I really had a bad, sleepless, pain-filled night!

Mick and Mack have been suspended indefinitely. Their parents have put them under curfew, and they have to have home study. I wish it was legal to give them forty lashes and tie them up by their thumbs like we read about in one book, but, of course, that would be considered too uncivilized and barbaric. I wonder if they realize how barbaric and uncivilized their actions were to me.

I finally consented to come back to school on Monday because it's Doodle Day, where the teachers try to do what the kids want for a change. At first I thought I couldn't; then at noon, Lew and "his harem"—as some of his tennis team still call us— telephoned, and I guess I'll heal from that horrible experience too, but I'm not sure.

Friday, April 12

5:45 P.M.

I guess all the kids at school heard what happened, because most of them were *extra nice* to me. I suspect Mrs. Maggleby or the principal talked to them over the loudspeaker, but maybe it just came through the grapevine. Anyway, I wish they'd just treat me like they treat everybody else. I want to be *JUST ME,* not the girl with AIDS!

10:10 P.M.

Sometimes I wonder if the kids are nice to me just because they're glad I'm not them! I wonder if they wonder if they might have HIV too. Cheese, I wonder if any of them do. I remember how some of the guys used to brag about having "done the deed," thinking it was macho and stuff. And everyone's always called Nelly Sivers "Loosie Goosie," seeing her around with real old guys. This is a nice, clean little town ... but is it possible that some of our kids have it and won't know for years and years and years? Maybe I'm lucky that my immune system is so low that I knew after less than a year ... or am I? Life is so, so, so, so complicated, isn't it?

Wednesday, April 24

7:17 P.M.

The last week or more have been so busy and dizzy I haven't had time or energy to write. School will be out in 44 days, and Red and El and Dorie and I have been trying to get all the life into our lives that we can push, pull, shove, take or make ... at least Dorie and I have—for different reasons, to be sure. It's hard to believe that in about four months Dorie will be a mother. Imagine, Dorie a mom to a real live 24-hour-a-day needing-care baby. I'm glad we had Mom's sister's baby, Bonny, with us that time. It really gave me a different perspective about babies, especially since a big apartment-house deal came up for Mom and *I* had to do most of the care-giving. It might have been different if Mom had been home, and I could just have played with the little kid when I wanted to. That doesn't mean that I don't someday want Lew's and my children, just not when I'm still a kid myself. Adults are different; they don't mind doing diapers, changing wet diapers, giving baths, dressing, and then it's time to start over. Poor Dorie. Anyway, she's having fun now. She just wears her blouses on the outside and wears bigger shorts and pants.

Me, I just do my thing, hit every bathroom or ladies' room within sight. I think my kidneys are about the size of peanuts . . . oh a joke . . . not very ha-ha, though.

Tuesday, May 7

11:20 A.M.

Can you believe it, El is having a Birthday Party for *ME*. I'm so excited. She is inviting *TWENTY KIDS,* and we're going to have a barbecue at her house, then go to a movie, then come home and dance on their volleyball court. I can't wait. I SIMPLY CANNOT WAIT! Time has stopped still in its tracks. I guess I love dancing with Lew more than anything in this whole world, more even than Baskin Robbins Pralines and Cream ice cream! One time I asked Dorie, after we'd seen the sexy part of *Ghost,* when she was sleeping over, what sex was really like, and she giggled and said, "Better than 31 flavors Pralines and Cream ice cream." I'm glad she said that, because Pralines and Cream is about as good as it can get at this point in my life. I know it's dumb and infantile, but I think of *it* every time I have some.

6:30 P.M.

After work, Mom bought me this darling pink pantsuit. It's got a big, bright-colored parrot on the front with long blue-and-red feathers dangling to the waist. I love it. LOVE IT, *LOVE IT!* And she bought me these really nice sandals just exactly the same shade of bright dark blue as the parrot feathers, and a big chiffon bow for my hair. I know Lew will love it. I hope he still loves me. I wonder if he really does .... if he can. It really scares me when I honestly look at myself deep inside. I'm soooo, so painfully exhausted all the time, and I have to push myself hard to do all the things that the other kids do with ease. Often when I go to the bathroom, I just lie on the floor with my feet up against the wall for a couple of minutes to try and get myself tied back together, even when it's a kind of icky place with no privacy. Oh well, I've always been kind of a sickly kid ... but how come some people have lots of years before the HIV virus turns to full-blown AIDS? Okay, Scarlett, *"think about that tomorrow."* I've got to read *that* book, but it's so biggggggg. I guess I'll do that too some "tomorrow" or the next day.

Whatever Day

8:27 P.M.

All the kids who are coming to MY birthday party are as excited as I am. We meet in the halls and giggle and jump up and down. Even the guys are acting goony. It's been a long, long time since the last really *something* party, which this will be. El's parents really know how to do things up right and bright. They're even renting the bus that looks like a trolley to take us to the movie and bring us back. Isn't that the most mag thing you've ever heard? Lew and I are going to sit on the backseat. That was his idea! I wonder what he has in mind. I wish it was what I have in mind, but it probably isn't. Besides, I didn't *really* even mean that! I don't think he'd even kiss me in public, but who knows ... maybe. His relatives are all very physical, kissing and hugging and bugging us. I like that. That's the way we're going to be.

Thursday, May 9

10:05 P.M.

It seems like it's been Thursday FOREVER. Won't Thursday ever go away. I want it to be Friday ... NOW ... NOW ... NOW. I've fantasized every moment. Well, gotta go start dinner. Mom will be home early. She's got a night appointment to close a deal. I hope it goes through; they don't always. 'Bye.

Cross your fingers, Self, so Friday will come faster, okay?

Friday, May 10

5:30 A.M.

I've got to go back to sleep. I've put out all my clothes and puttered around for about an hour. I'll probably fall asleep over dinner with my face in the barbecue. Not likely with Lew around! But I really had better start relaxing and concentrating on my slow breathing in and out and nothing else. That is supposed to work to get people to sleep.

Good night ... er ... well ... whatever.

Tonight is *really* going to be the *Good* night!! Imagine, me sixteen! Old enough to *date!* Old enough to *drive!*

5:30 P.M.

I've washed and rewashed my hair and put it up 37 different ways, but I still look a mess. I wanted to look my very best, and here I am with a yick on my forehead like Mount Vesuvius about to erupt. Lew might see me and run. I hope Mom will be able to help me cover it with makeup. I think she can. She's very good with those things. Besides, I'm definitely going to wear bangs, at least on that side. I'll have Mom trim some. I wonder if I can take Mom with me when I get married. Sometimes I can't wait to get away, and then other times, like this minute, it's . . . I don't know . . . I'm such a loony tune, retard, jerk sometimes.

6:30 P.M.

I'm going nuts. Where can Mom be? I hope she hasn't had an accident or something. She said she'd be home early. We have to leave in *49 minutes,* and she's got to trim a little bang and put the magic makeup on before that. I'm all dressed and going crazy. Where could she be? Maybe she had a heart attack, or maybe she was showing a house to some weirdo and . . . *that's* really out in coo-coo land . . . but those things happen. Cheese, I wonder if this is how she worries about me when I'm a little late or something. I never thought about that.

Oops, I hear her key in the door.

Wish me luck and kisses and everything, especially kisses, right? RIGHT?

I'll probably be up all night telling you every little delicious detail. I will. I promise.

Oh, dearest of dear Self:

I'm so glad, so thankful, so appreciative that I have *you*. Who else could I turn to? I couldn't possibly tell Mom. It would be too hurtful to her. It's bad enough as it is. My problem has hurt her more than any mother should ever, ever be hurt. *Poor* Mom ... poor me ... poor, poor Mom ... poor, poor, poor me.

But back to the very beginning. The party started out so wonderfully. Lew was there when I arrived, and he was waiting for me. I got shivers just seeing him in his blue pants and his blue-and-white-check shirt. It is a sight that is permanently locked into my brain, him smiling like he was seeing sunshine and color for the first time, his cowlick sticking up like always, and his little blond front curl hanging down in his left eye. What a celestial-planet sight. Oh, and everybody else was there too. El had asked them to come at 6:15. They all yelled, "HAPPY BIRTHDAY," and threw confetti and those long paper streamers at me that are usually only used on New Year's. But I guess this is the beginning of a New Year. I'm sixteen! I can't believe it. Then everyone picked the confetti out of my hair and off my clothes. I felt like Princess Di or someone especially special.

El's dad, who is the best sport in the world, started a tape and then a conga line. We weaved and weaved around the patio furniture and the volleyball area and bushes and trees and stuff, going faster and faster until people were falling down on top of one another. I'd have fallen a dozen times if Lew hadn't stopped me. Then El's dad told me I was to choose one "little girl's game" before I was officially a sixteen-year-old young woman.

Everyone started yelling: Jacks, Spin the Bottle, Post Office, Jump Rope, all the night games, but I decided on Pretty or Ugly. You know, where you spin someone till they are dizzy, then tell them they have to look like whatever statue you call at the last minute.

It was sooooo fun and funny. Red fell down in a crazy awkward sprawl, and Mark called "Pretty" just as he let go. We all almost cried, we were laughing so hard. Lew was very gentle with me and called "Pretty" like I knew he would. He is so sweet and mature. He said I couldn't look ugly if I tried. Isn't that precious and unteenage boylike? But I guess that's not so strange. All of his relatives are respectful of themselves and everybody else. It's a wonderful thing I'm trying to put into my own life.

The barbecue was mag, even though El did burn her arm on the grill, and they had to stop and get ice and stuff, and Donny's drink popped up and showered his face and hair and got some on Delta, who is the prissiest thing in the world. You would have thought he had tarred and feathered her. She wanted to call her mom to come and get her so she could change her clothes, but El's mom finally cleaned her off and cooled her down. I spilled a mixture of mustard and catsup down the front of my shirt, as usual, when it squished out the end of my hamburger, but Lew said it blended with my parrot feathers, and when I looked in the mirror, sure enough it did.

Does Lew control not only my heart but my brain and eyesight as well?

The movie was really funny. Lew put his arm around me and held my hand and I was in heaven.

They could have shown the worst movie in the world, and I would have loved, loved, loved every second of it.

All twenty of us were laughing and being silly, and I suspect all the other people in the audience hated us, but we didn't care. At least Lew and I didn't care. We were being very quiet and wonderful. I felt like making the nice little sounds that birds make when they're comfortably settling down in their nests for the night . . . or that kittens make when you're petting them in front of an open fire. I wanted the movie to never, never end.

Two or three times Lew reached over and kissed me quickly on the cheek or ear. It was like the Mormon Tabernacle Choir began singing the "Hallelujah" chorus. Every molecule in my body stood up at attention with their hands across their hearts—that is, they would have if they had hands and hearts.

Uhhhhhh . . . this part is even hard to write. I hope I can dump it all on you and never think of it again . . . wouldn't that be wonderful. Maybe someday they'll have a FORGET pill. I hope so. Anyway, I was sitting there in the movie, leaning on Lew's shoulder and purring as contently as any creature ever could . . .

AND IT HAPPENED . . .
IT *JUST HAPPENED!!!!!*

Often in the last few weeks I've had to make dashes to the bathroom—at school, at home, or wherever—but this . . . I had ABSOLUTELY NO CONTROL. I jumped up and started squeezing my way down the row, facing people so I could push them away. As I got to the aisle, I was so humiliated I wanted to faint, disappear, die ... die ... die ...

Sixteen-year-old women *do not wet their pants* in a movie theater with nineteen of their friends around them. It took all the control I could muster to keep from bawling out loud. Thank everything good for the darkness.

I got to the door of the lobby, but there was no way I could go out there. There were gobs of people milling around at the candy counter, including El and Dan. I had one mad moment of wondering what would happen if I crashed the Exit door. Maybe they'd turn on the house lights and EVERYONE, *EVERYONE* IN THE WHOLE PLACE, WOULD WITNESS MY HUMILIATION ... MY PAIN, MY SHAME. There was no way I could handle that.

In spite of my fears, I dashed for the Exit door. It opened with no big problem except starting some blinking lights and strange buzzing, but by that time I didn't care. I was in the alley and running toward a bunch of trash cans and cardboard boxes. Without a second thought, I crept into the stinking mess and curled up as small as I could and close to the ground.

I could hear two male voices cursing in the distance, saying that a stupid kid probably had tried to let in some buddies for free ... then all became quiet. I had no idea of what I was going to do, but I knew that there was no way I would leave my hidey-hole until I was sure the kids had all left the movie. I peeked out and could see that a line for the next show was beginning to queue up, so I knew it wouldn't be long. Trying not to breathe in case Lew or some of the others came looking for me, I stayed absolutely quiet.

After a little while, I began to hear soft, moving

noises. They got louder and louder, scratching in paper and squeaking. Automatically I knew there were *RATS* in and around the cans! My heart fluttered and vomit spurted up in my throat. I told myself again that I wouldn't move, no matter what, but when I felt something scurry across my leg, I couldn't bear it and hurriedly squeezed out from between the cans.

Hugging the black wall, I dashed for the opposite end of the alley, which looked miles away. Once on the street, I noticed it was much dimmer lit than Main Street, where the movie house was, and there was very little traffic. I wondered if any cabby in his right mind would stop for a kid who probably looked like she'd just crawled out of a garbage heap, because she had.

The only thing good was I'd crawled through something brown, so you couldn't tell that ... you know ... *that* was soooooooo horrific. I wish I knew an even more horrible word ... sitting there in Lew's arms and realizing what was happening. Oh, dear God, I hope I jumped up in time so the seat wasn't all wet. Ruining my pants I can take, but ... please, please ... don't let anyone else know.

Anyway, after forever a cab came by and stopped. I was waving hysterically and was halfway out into the street—not caring if I got hit or not, actually hoping in a way that I would get hit; then I wouldn't need explanations or apologies or anything. This way ... I don't know ... *this* is worse than AIDS or anything!

I will thank you God, forever, for having Mom make me keep a ten-dollar bill in my purse at all times. I've kept one curled up for years in my little zipper pocket and never needed it UNTIL NOW!

Oh, thank you, Mom; thank you, God. Thank you both.

The cabby thought I'd been date-dumped in the garbage cans in the alley, and he wanted to take me to the police station or the rape center, but I said I had to go home first, and my mom would take me.

He was a nice, caring man who had three daughters of his own, and he made me promise I'd go and not take a bath or anything so they could check the guy's semen, which, he said, is as reliable as a fingerprint, isn't that weird?

Thank goodness Mom wasn't home. Maybe I'll tell her tomorrow . . . maybe I won't.

Oh yes, I had enough common sense to call El's mom.

I told her I'd gotten sick in the movie and come home in a cab. She said El had just called her from the movie and that she'd call her back and explain. I'm so grateful she didn't scold me or lecture me or any of that other mother stuff that is so brain-frying.

First I came home and showered and washed my hair and put my clothes in a plastic bag; then I cried all my tears out, and wrote all my heart out. Now, now I'll just . . . what? There are no more tears and there are *no* solutions . . . I think I'll take two or three aspirin or Tylenol or whatever Mom has in her medicine cabinet. I've got to escape some way.

Dear Mary, Mother of God, please listen to me. No one in the whole world has ever been in such deep anguish . . . please . . . please.

12:21 A.M.

It is a miracle. My prayers really were heard. Right at the point where I honestly thought I was going to disintegrate or something from the pain, the phone rang. It was dear, caring, thoughtful Lew. He was sur-

145

prised when I answered, and he told me how bad he felt that my birthday party had been ruined by something I'd eaten or whatever. I told him I'd been up-chucking and upchucking, but that I felt a lot better now that he had called. That one little tiny, weenie part was true.

I told him I hoped the kids had gone on with the party and that I hadn't spoiled everything for them. He said they had as soon as El's mom called back and said I was all right.

It was so wonderful to hear him and to know that no one knew about my . . . accident. I was glad they were all dancing to the little combo from El's dad's office and having all the fun they were entitled to.

I wanted Lew to stay on the phone forever, but he said I had to go back to bed and rest. I can do that too, because his last words were, "Take care of yourself, my little Nancy, because you are sacredly precious to me." Isn't that beautiful from a sixteen-year-old boy? Elizabeth Barrett Browning, move over. "Sacredly precious." Those two beautiful words beautifully put together are emblazoned on my heart in pastel neon permanently.

Monday, May 13

10:13 A.M.

I was almost happy to go see Dr. S. this morning. I was hoping he'd be able to do something about the kidney thing, but he was so busy, one of the nurses took care of me. It seems like every time I go to his office there are more and more people, but that, of course, is just paranoid *me*. I'm getting more and more paranoid about everything in life! Anyway, the

146

nurse just gave me a box of Depends and told me to use them till I got to see Dr. S. I thought I'd die right there. Diapers, me? Me, sixteen years and two days old? Only old, old, old people and little babies wear diapers! I wouldn't do it. I simply wouldn't. I refused to even take them from her hand and walked out.

Mom was in the waiting room, and I told her everything was fine. What a great liar I've become.

12:57 P.M.

Mom dropped me off at the apartment because I said I was exhausted. The phone was ringing when I walked in, and I don't know why I picked up the phone, because I certainly didn't feel like talking to anyone, but I did anyway.

I can't understand why Dorie has to see me immediately. She says it's really, really, important. I do hope nothing bad is happening to her or the baby after all this time, or to Jake. He's been her next-door neighbor since before they were born, and he's more like a brother than anything. He's been so protective of her; even at the party when everyone was playing Pretty or Ugly, he pretended he just wanted to sit and watch so she would. I've got some really dear friends here. I guess *maybe* I can stand what I have to stand.

Actually, Self, I haven't even been absolutely honest with you. I've been sort of . . . wetting the bed for the last couple of weeks. It's been too embarrassing to even admit, but I guess I might as well. I have to get up and change my bedclothes and put them in the washer with a lot of Clorox bleach and stuff. You know . . . body fluids . . . and all that. I worry about "body fluids" and the movie thing too. What if . . .

oh, how I wish I could contact someone who knows something every time I have a question.

But skip reality. I've got to go into fantasy to save my sanity. A buttercupped meadow, me and Lew, nothing else through endless time. . . .

3:45 P.M.

Dorie pushed her way in as soon as I'd opened the door. It was obvious she had run all the way from the bus stop like demons were chasing her. Once she got inside the door, we hugged each other like we would never let go, and we cried and cried, mixed tears of joy and tears of sorrow. My fears and joys were hers and hers were mine. We were one in our friendship. It was both splendid and sad at the same time.

After a while we just sat on the floor and looked at each other. I knew she had something to say, but it wouldn't come out. Finally, in the voice and posture of a guru or someone who could control both our emotions, she quietly told me why she was there. It was like she was someone else detached from the whole thing and so was I.

It seems Delta suspected what had happened when I jostled out of the row and up the aisle. And when the movie was over and the lights were up, she pretended she'd left her purse and went back and touched the seat. It was wet! The rest of the evening she and Marcie completely ignored the other kids at the party and sat in corners or huddled together giggling.

By Sunday afternoon *EVERYBODY* in town was whispering about my having *"wet my pants"* in the movie and having gone home, later telling everybody that I'd gotten sick.

At first it was like Dorie was talking about some other poor, helpless kid; then it hit me, and I collapsed in a heap. Dorie felt terrible, but she had felt she had to tell me, and she was right. It was much better and kinder than ... than ... whatever else there was to do. She helped me get to bed, gave me an aspirin and left.

Dear Self, no one in the whole world has ever been so embarrassed and humiliated. Oh, dear God, I want to die *now*, not weeks from now, or months from now, or even years from now. Please, please, God, let me die this very minute. I can bear the pain, but I *can't* bear the shame. I am soooooo alone and helpless. No one in the world is sooooo alone and helpless.

Thursday, May 16

6:30 P.M.

I have not been out of my room for three days, and I will not let Mom open my drapes. I want it black on the outside of me. As black as it is on the inside of me, black and filled with nothing nothingness. My mind is black and stuck and won't work. It's protective in there, and I'm going to keep it that way.

Mom offered to take me down to get my driver's license, but even that doesn't sound worth doing.

? Day

? Time

I guess it's been a week or so since ... you know. Mom says if I don't eat they're going to take me to the hospital and put an IV in me. But I won't go. No one can make me.

SOMETIME—WHO KNOWS ... WHO CARES ...

Mom says she's taking me to Arizona to stay with Dad. That the dry desert air and all the sunshine will make me feel better. I don't want to go ... I WANT TO DIE ... but I'm scared ... I don't want to. That's so dumb. *Maybe* they will find a cure for AIDS *soon*. Dr. S. called and said he feels they're pretty close. He begged me to hang on. . . . I don't know if it's worth it. Do you think it is? Well, okay, I guess I will, then.

9:10 P.M.

Mom keeps begging me to take the kids' phone calls ... but I can't. I really, honestly *can't!* I can't even talk to Dorie now for some reason. I don't want to! I won't! What is there to say?

Sunday, May 19

4:02 P.M.

We're in Phoenix. I'm exhausted. I had no idea I was so weak. I actually had to be helped on and off the plane.

Wednesday, May 22

10:40 P.M.

Mom's gone home and Dad has lovingly but firmly told me that if I don't eat every two hours, he is going to take me directly to the hospital. I don't want that, so I guess I'll try. I'll do it for him. He looks so hurt and sad ... and so did Mom. How selfish I've been not to think of them one single bit ... only myself . . . always me . . . me . . . me. They've got pains and strains too.

Saturday, May 25

9:22 A.M.

Maria, Dad's housekeeper, is really nice. She speaks very little English, and my Spanish is *malo*. We're having fun teaching each other. I wish I had listened more carefully and studied harder in my Spanish class.

Mom made a list of all the things I like, and Maria tries hard to fix them, but they all taste a little different than when Mom did it. Anyway, I'm eating every two hours, and I'm walking around the pool and out into the cactus garden. It's beautiful here, especially in the early morning when the sun comes up. It's like God's glorious head is slowly rising up over the mountains. It's almost sacred. I remember one time Dad took me to an Indian festival. I was really impressed because everything is sacred to them: trees and sand and sun and water and people and animals and even rocks and stuff. Maybe Dad will take me to one again. I hope so.

Wednesday, May 29

12:32 P.M.

I'm feeling so much better I can't believe it. Maria is having a big Spanish lunch at one o'clock out in the patio. Dad has invited his friend Liz. I can't wait to meet her, and I can't wait to eat. I'm starving . . . starving . . . starving.

I wonder if Liz is as pretty as Mom, as nice as

Mom, as concerned as Mom. Some nasty little part inside me hopes that she isn't, but I guess that I hope that she is too, for Dad's sake. I don't think I can ever like her, but I'll try. After all, Mom and Dad have been divorced over two years now.

5:02 P.M.

I tried hard not to like Liz, but I like her anyway. She's just the opposite of Mom, tall and bronze with dark hair and almost black eyes.

After lunch, we put on our swimsuits, and Dad and Liz splashed me when they went into the pool, but no matter how much they coaxed, I wouldn't go in. I'm not sure about "body fluids" and swimming pools. I wish there was a hot line of some kind. But I won't think about *that!!!*

Liz has a beautiful body, and she's so considerate and respectful of Dad and me and even Maria. It's like she's a real lady. Not that Mom isn't, but Liz is sort of regal or something. When she put on Dad's robe to go into the house for something, the wide belt was dragging along behind her like a train, and Dad had put some flowers in her hair that looked almost like a crown. I'm afraid I'm going to like her. She has an ad agency, and she's invited me to come down. In fact, she said she might even find me a part-time job there when I feel better. That *made* me feel better. Imagine ME with a part-time, wonderful, glorious, glamorous job!

2:30 P.M.

I like Liz so much that I almost feel like I'm being unfaithful to Mom. Is that possible? I wonder how much *I* had to do with their divorce. Again, maybe if I'd been more respectful and not so whiny, if I'd kept my room clean and done my chores, if I'd been nicer and sweeter and prettier, if . . . if . . . if.

Lots of questions in life and few answers.

Monday, June 3

2:30 P.M.

Liz just called and wants me to come in tomorrow. She'll have me interview with her office manager just like any other person.

It's scary, hairy scary.

What will I wear? How will I fix my hair? Will they like me? Sometimes I can be so dumb and klutsy. I don't want to embarrass Liz. I don't want to embarrass Dad. But I guess most of all I don't want to embarrass myself.

Maybe the office manager will be big and gruff and mean. Maybe she'll expect someone with lots of experience and confidence. Maybe she'll hate *everything* about me . . . but then, maybe she won't.

Midnight—Exactly

I've laid out my white dress trimmed with navy blue and my navy shoes. That outfit looks most like what Liz would wear. They've got to like me . . .

they've got to . . . they've got to. If only I didn't have to wear the damn diaper, but I'd better.

Tuesday, June 4

10:30 A.M.

Dad dropped me by Liz's office and told me not to worry, but my teeth were rattling as I walked into the building. Liz's office manager was as sweet and gentle as she is, and within minutes I knew I had the job.

I'm going to be kind of a "gofer," going for this and for that for anyone in the office and doing some filing and taking the desk while the receptionist takes breaks and stuff. I am *so* excited and elated, and everything wonderful and happy! Me! Me! With a glamorous job. Who would have thought it could happen? And Dad's taking me tomorrow to get my driver's license. Wow!

Thursday, June 27

6:22 P.M.

I've been working for 22 glorious days, almost a month! The summer is a third over. I've got to start thinking about school. Dad wants me to stay here and Liz says I can work part-time. Mom wants me to go there. I don't know what I want. I know I don't want to go back to my old school, but I don't want to hurt Mom, either. Oh well, I guess I'll worry about that tomorrow . . . or next never day. I've gotten even worse than Scarlett.

Saturday, June 29

8:30 A.M.

It's so mag to have my own check. Today I'm going to go out and buy something nice for Mom. I would love to buy something wonderful for Lew and the rest of the gaggle too, but I won't! That is a distant past part of my old live, like the divorce. I guess in a way I have divorced them. Sometimes those things have to be done!

Tuesday, July 2

6:02 P.M.

Today I had lunch with Adam again. It was funny how we met. He's mailroom boy for the building and my first day here I was getting off the elevator with my arms full, and he was getting on with his arms full, and we bumped into each other. Our stuff flew everywhere, mixing itself together. By the time we had sorted everything out and apologized and apologized and apologized, we felt like old-time buddies.

Adam is sooo nice. He's in high school, and he wants to become a dentist like his dad. He's very serious and reserved. He said he'd been watching me since the first day I came, but was too shy to say anything. I teased him then and accused him of bumping into me on purpose. That was the first time I've ever seen a boy blush. It's the first time I've ever had enough self-confidence to be a little bit aggressive too. IT FEELS GOOD!

I don't know why I haven't told you about Adam before. Maybe I was afraid it would mean bad luck for Lew and me, or some crazy other something.

Anyway, Adam is a lot like Kyle, Lew's brother, don't you think so?

Friday, July 12

10:54 P.M.

Adam has a car. His *very own* car. It isn't much, but it's his! Maybe someday I'll have a car. I can't wait. There is no way Dad will let me drive his Porsche by myself—only when he's with me.

Adam and I went to an Indian lecture. Then we went and had pizza. It was Dutch. I'm a liberated woman now, and I want Adam for a friend-friend, not a boyfriend. It's so much more comfortable.

Monday, August 5

Dear Self:

I have a secret that I can only tell to you. I think I'm getting better, I really do. The fact is I KNOW I'M BETTER! I work all day at the office; then Adam and I do something a couple of nights a week. They have lots of wonderful things to do here, so we don't always have to go to movies. They have pop and rock concerts by not-so-well-known people all the time, and some of the groups are really good. Adam plays wind instruments. His dad used to play with a name band when he was young; now the three of us get together and just have fun. Mr. Alred has taught me to read chord music. It's really hot, and it wasn't that hard. He says I'm "naturally talented," but I think he just says that because I'm Adam's friend. Still, I must remember "the sin of ingratitude" and be appreciative. Aunt Thelma says I'm "gifted" with art. *I know* she's partial, but just between the

156

two of us, I think maybe I'm pretty good too. Is that being conceited? If it is, don't tell anybody. Okay? Okay.

Adam and I like the live plays here too. He says next summer he'll try out for one if I will. Maybe we should. Maybe we will! I guess I'll stay here and go to school.

2:15 A.M.

Dear Self:
I know you want me to talk to you more about Mom and the gaggle, but I can't, I really can't. It hurts too much. If I pretend *they're pretend,* it's easier. I know that sounds dumb and childish and all that, but please give me a little more time. Okay?

Sometimes when I think about Lew, he seems more unreal than real, like maybe I dreamed him up or something. It scares me that they all seem so dim . . . but whatever . . . I can't handle their ghosts in my life right now. Okay?

I have to talk to Mom every Sunday when she calls, and she's been here three times, but I can't read the letters the kids send, not yet.

I'm bawling like the floodgates to my soul and hell have broken open, vomiting up all my pain. You see, I can't seem to separate the good from the bad right now. Please, please don't make me try again. It hurts less if I detach myself.

Friday, August 9

We've named ourselves the Almost All Red Aborigines, and Adam's mom is playing the bass guitar with us. His dad says she used to be a hippie, but of course he's kidding. But maybe he isn't, because

she's taught us some of the almost classic old songs
they did in those days, and we're going to play them
at her class reunion. Doesn't that sound like the
greatest? I didn't know old people could be so much
fun. Well, they're not *really* old, but then they are
too.

We invited Dad and Liz and a few people from the
office over to the Alreds' for a party, and we played.
They all went crazy, even Dad. It was fun to watch
old (well, lots older than we are) people loosen up
and get with the music. Mr. Alred bought a little electric piano so we could move it out by the pool. That's
super cool, because now I can watch all the action.

Monday, August 19

We've had two paid gigs since the office party.
Adam's mom and dad play for fun and give Adam
and me all the money for our college funds. Last
night at a party for a local club, three men who used
to be in bands when they were young sat in with us.
It was a blast. We had others coming up to sing the
lyrics. Some were good, some were so-so and one
guy was terrible. In fact, he was so bad he was funny.
He acted really serious and everybody howled and
clapped and clapped. Most of them even stopped
dancing and just egged him on.

Tuesday, August 20

6:15 P.M.

At dinner Dad was grinning like a mean little kid.
He said he had a surprise for me, and even though I
whined and teased and begged and coaxed and sat on
his lap and pouted like I used to do when I was a

spoiled little bratty boob, he wouldn't tell me what it was. We're really getting close, and I love it.

Friday, August 23

2:30 A.M.

Pinch me, Self. I think I'm dreaming. I came in from work early and piddled around the kitchen like I usually do, then went into my room to get into some shorts and guess what? El was flopped out on my bed like she belonged there. I was so surprised I almost wet . . . erase . . . For a moment we just looked at each other. Then we hugged like we'd never let go. I don't know when I've ever been so happy. My heart was flopping around inside me like a goldfish out of water on the floor. We both started talking at once, laughing and giggling and squealing like we had in grade school. I'm sure Dad could have heard us at his office downtown.

Dad came home and took us out to dinner; then we scrambled back into my room to talk some more. Dad came in about eleven to warn us not to stay up all night and giggle, but I knew from the look on his face the he knew we'd do it anyway. He kissed us and tucked us in like we were ga-ga's. It was wonderful. El is the sister I've never had, and I love her with every atom of my self. I don't know how I could have tried so hard to cut her, and the rest of the gaggle, out of my life for so long. What a coo-coo I've been for not letting them in when I needed them most.

They've written me long letters and sent pictures and called, and I've just tried to pretend they didn't exist, never phoning and only returning say-nothing notes. What a nutso fruitcake I've been. I love them and admire them and need them completely. I apologized and apologized to El, and she just gave me a nogie and a face squish and told me she was glad I'd finally gotten my beans together.

I don't know when she's going back, but I hope it's not for a long, long, long time, because it's going to take forever for us to catch up on everything. But let me fill you in on a few things.

Dorie had her baby August 22. It was a girl! She gave it to a nice couple in California who have been trying to have children for seven years. The lady is twenty-eight and the man is thirty. They have a nice home, and he's the manager of a pro golf shop. It's sad, but it isn't sad too. Everybody wants what's best for "Little Dorie." I don't care what those people name her, she'll always be "Little Dorie" to El and me.

Lew has spent most of the summer working with his uncle in Raleigh. El says he always wears my CHK ring on a chain around his neck. It got too small for his finger; rather, his finger grew too big for the ring. That makes me embarrassed because I haven't worn his ring since I got here. Maybe I'll put it back on ... think I should? Think I dare?

Red is still Red. I miss her *so much!*

My mom, El says, just seems sort of "gray" since I left. She smiles every time they meet, but only her outside smiles, not her inside. I wish I could remember exactly how El explained it, but anyway, I get the picture, and I feel sooooo selfish and self-centered. I haven't been thinking about her pain and strain and fears and tears at all, only about my own. Maybe I should go home for school. So I did wet my pants in the theater. It's my word against Delta's, and by now everyone's probably forgotten anyhow. It would be fun to be home for Halloween and Thanksgiving and Christmas. Oh, I want to wake El up and talk about it, but she's sound asleep making little kitten kinds of purring noises. I'd forgotten how neat they sound.

Monday, August 26

El had to go back Sunday, and I miss her more than I thought possible. It's like part of my body has been amputated. She says the gaggle is hoping and praying I'll come back for school. How could anyone resist that? Dad had it set up with Liz to let me take off while El was here, and we haven't been apart one minute except to go to the bathroom. Even then one time El started jumping up and down outside the door, banging and yelling, "Hurry up, hurry up, I'm lonely, and we can't waste any time apart." I came out, and we fell on the floor laughing till we cried. It was like the good old days.

Tuesday, August 27

9:10 P.M.

After work Adam and I went to the mall, then had pizza and took in a movie. I love him in a sacred, comfortable, friendly way, but he'll *never* take the place of any member of the gaggle. Sometimes we hold hands or he puts his arm around me, but I don't get goose bumps and that warm, glowing feeling that overwhelms me when Lew does the same thing. El assured me that Lew doesn't have another girl, but . . .

If I didn't have . . . it . . . I'd go home in a minute. Please, please, Self, tell me what to do.

What's best for me? . . . for Lew? . . . for everybody? It's kind of like with Dorie and Little Dorie . . . sometimes the main person isn't the main person at all! Maybe I should just think about Lew and let him get on with his life. But then again, maybe I should go have a checkup and take it from there. It would really be nice to be home for Mom's birthday, September 27. Maybe I could even have a surprise party for her. We could have it in the clubhouse, and maybe I could get together a little combo like we have here.

2:47 A.M.

This is really strange. My own whimpering woke me up. I was dreaming about how much I loved my precious forever mama and how achingly lonely I was for her. I'm a part of her. I grew from a tiny egg inside her warm body. For the first time since I came to Dad's, I am allowing myself to feel the true warm wonder of our holy relationship. It's so comforting and protective and belonging—and I want to go home! Home! Home! I've *got* to go home! I don't want to cut Mom out of my life anymore.

I'll talk to Liz the first thing in the morning; I'll call Mom as soon as it's a decent calling hour, or maybe even while it's an indecent hour—so there.

Wednesday, August 28

7:15 A.M.

I was just getting ready to call Mom, even though it's earlier there than here, when I remembered that Trudy broke her arm last week. I can't just up and quit Liz when she's been so nice to me and she needs me so much and has shuffled things so I can work

162

part-time after school starts. I can't do all of Trudy's work, but I can do enough of it so that Beth can cover. I wonder how long it takes an arm to heal. Something tells me it's six weeks, but I *can't wait* five whole long weeks more. Oh, garbage, why couldn't it have been me? The office can get by without *me,* but not without her.

I guess I'll just have to wait and talk to Dad tonight, but I know he's as mixed up as I am. I often hear him crying in the night. I'm hurting everybody I love sooooo much!

Thursday, August 29

6:17 P.M.

Dad talked to Liz, and she's going to try to get someone as soon as possible. I guess I can live with that, especially since Dad said I can call Mom and El tonight and tell them I'm going to come back there for school, even if it's a little late.

Friday, August 30

11:01 P.M.

Dear Self:

Our Arizona high school classes start Tuesday ... four more days ... four more spooky days. Adam had driven me by where I'll go, but today we got out and wandered around. It isn't the high school he goes to, but they do have competitions against each other sometimes. He thinks I'll like the kids and the teachers and everything. I'm so excited and S-C-A-R-E-D, but I try to think about proms and stuff. I dreamed for one moment about inviting Lew here; then I remembered I won't be here by then! I'LL BE *THERE!* WOW! WOWIE! MAG! MAGNIF! MAGNIFICENT! I can handle a week or so here, or can I?

Sunday, September 1

Dad and I went to Mass just to give me some courage for Tuesday. Then I took hours deciding what I'd wear to my first day of school. I don't want to look too fancy, but then I don't want to look dowdy either. Kids can be pretty cruel . . . cruel if you're not wearing the cool "in" thing.

Friday, September 6

6:21 P.M.

I've been trying not to be negative, but I can't stand it anymore. I simply can't keep all the hostility bottled up inside myself, I'll explode! I HATE THIS SCHOOL! I DETEST AND LOATHE IT!! It's like I'm invisible. I can be walking through the halls with hundreds of kids on every side, and no one even sees me. I didn't know how lonely a person could feel when she is part of a scurrying mass of strangers— part of, but *not* part of! It's much, much, much more lonely than it ever could be being alone!

For one moment just before lunch, when I knew I'd have to eat by myself again in the cafeteria, I wanted to jump up and down and scream, I'VE GOT AIDS. I'VE GOT AIDS. I'VE GOT AIDS. Then they would have paid attention to me, I bet. Later, when I was sitting at my desk in English, I daydreamed of slumping over and dying a slow, tortuous death so they each could see how much their ignoring me hurt. Can't they . . . don't they know that unreal pain hurts almost more than real pain? But how could they know, when *I* didn't even know it until now?

They couldn't hurt me more with bats and chains and knives. I've never given a thought to new kids before. I grew up with most of the gaggle since kindergarten, most of the other kids too, and I've always belonged. I didn't realize how much being an outsider can hurt, how humiliating and ego-battering it is. Dear God, I promise from now on I will be considerate and kind to every stranger I meet, except possibly dangerous ones on the street and stuff, of course. Maybe, God, you wanted this to happen to me so I'd have a chance to see and feel what it's like to *not* belong. It has, believe me, taught a lesson I'll never forget and I don't need any more of. Please, please, no more.

I called a home teacher and asked if she could come to Dad's, but she said she can't if I'm well enough to go to regular school. Well? I'm body "well," but more heart and emotions sick than I've ever been!

How can society do this? I want t die, but dying is not *that* easy, so I guess I'll call Adam and spill my guts out to him. Please, God, let him be home.

Saturday, September 7

6:45 P.M.

I woke up so tired I could hardly force myself up to go to the bathroom. I guess I've been burning my black negative candles at both ends, whatever that means.

I've pushed myself all day just to do the things that

I usually do unconsciously. I'm going to bed as soon as I fix myself something to eat.

Monday, September 9

5:30 P.M.

This is kind of scary. I've gotten ten hours' sleep for the last two nights and taken a nap each day, and I still feel, and I guess act, exhausted, because even Dad and Adam have noticed it.

Oh, please, dear God, not *it* now, not *it* again.

Tuesday, September 10

I guess I'm depressed about not being able to go home, because I'm feeling more lumpy and grumpy every day. A few kids have started treating me like I'm an earth-being and not from another planet, but that doesn't heal the past pain. Isn't it funny that new kids are either accepted as prime-time attractions or as *nothings?* I wonder if it's true of adults. I think not! It's too immature.

Wednesday, September 11

4:10 P.M.

For the last few days I've stayed in bed every minute I wasn't at work or school, but I feel lumpier and grumpier than ever, anyway. I don't know how I'm possibly going to handle both school and work tomorrow, even though it's my *last day!* Then I'm outta here! Goody-bye, Arizona!

My chest hurts, my arms hurt, my legs hurt, even my hair and my toenails hurt. I told Dad I was just taking my last licks at being lazy, but something deep inside tells me that it's more than that! I guess I should have called Dr. Marx. He's the doctor in Phoenix that Dr. Sheranian told me to see as soon as I got here, but I've felt so good I didn't need him till now. I think this is only the flu, but . . .

7:10 P.M.

When Dad got home he immediately called Dr. Marx. Dr. M. said Dr. Sheranian had told him about me and that he'd see me as soon as I could get in.

Dr. Marx is black, and he's *so* young I thought he was an aide of some kind. He's funny, and he's so unplastic that I liked him immediately. He works in a nice little clinic, and he sent Dad out of the room as though he were the child instead of me. Me he treats "with the utmost respect and reverence" because "I am a member of the superior sex." His nurses snickered when he said that, and he picked up a male urinal, held it high, waved it around and said it was his scepter and that he knew what he was saying and doing. Then he assured me that he'd call Dad when he had finished running all the tests he wanted, which might take some time. I'm glad I remembered to stick you in my bag, Self. It would have been a dull, long evening without you.

They've punched and probed and X-rayed and shot me. Dr. Marx says he thinks I have an infection. I hope that's all it is, because *that* they can clear up with antibiotics in no time.

9:45 P.M.

Not my kind of infection they can't. It's AIDS-related and . . . all the evils of my past and future

167

have come back to haunt me. Maybe this is an omen that I *shouldn't* go back home . . . ever.

Tuesday, September 17

My home schoolteacher just left the clinic. He says I'm doing well with all my subjects and that I won't have any trouble homogenizing with my class when I get home. I thought "homogenize" was just something you did with milk, not people. I'm not sure I'd ever want to be *that* much a part of any of the people here, except, of course, Adam and Dad and Liz.

Wednesday, September 18

I've been well enough to go back to Mom's for ages, but Dr. Marx won't release me until he's "absolutely, positively, for sure certain" that my good bugs are in charge of my bad bugs.

Saturday, September 21

6:11 A.M.

I'm flying home at 2 P.M. this afternoon. I'm not sure I can wait that long. I'm so happy, happy, happy. I'll miss Dad a lot, and I'll miss Adam and his family too. They're like my second family. I've spent almost more time there than I have with Dad. I wish Dad was a dentist so he could just work certain hours and be through. He's a slave to his business. Adam's mom works two mornings a week in her husband's office, so she's always home with food and smiles and stuff when we go over there. I almost can't remember when Mom didn't work and I didn't have a couple of hours by myself after school before she got home. Life is really weird, isn't it? Nobody's ever got everything all good. It's like with Adam and his buddies; they're always talking about girls, but they never seem to go with them, so it's just me and Adam and them when we're together. I mostly just listen while they talk sports and rollerblades and stuff.

I'm realllllllly going to miss Adam, but the crap-happy school I'm going to erase completely out of my mind and never think about it again . . . I wish.

Thursday, October 31

1:32 A.M.—Halloween

Dearest dear Self:

I'm sorry I haven't written in you for so long, but you know you are ever in my heart, right? Right!

I have been so busy trying to catch up scholastically and socially and every other way that I've hardly had time to breathe. And I have been so contented, nurtured, loved, babied, spoiled and all the other good and belonging and happy words there are that . . . well, I promise I'll be better about writing in the future, okay? Am I forgiven? Thanks.

Tonight Lew and his buds had a party in Mr. Detmer's old barn. It was so scary that I'm sure people could hear us screaming in the next town. Jed's dad is a doctor, and he had IVs running into purple-and-green corpses. And there were headless people and arms and stuff that the guys must have gotten at a costume place or made out of papier-mâché or something, and they must have used *gallons* of catsup.

Lew took me through the spook alley, and I was

hanging on to him like I've been wanting to do for ages, although not in that exact setting.

After we'd eaten their gross menu

> *Hot dogs with blood (catsup)*
> *Green toe-jam (chopped pickles)*
> *Throw-up (mustard)*
> *Sunburned skin peel (potato chips)*
> *Arsenic (apple cider)*
> *Mud pies (marshmallow brownies)*

we danced, and I thought I'd gone to Heaven.

I couldn't believe it when a big gong sounded once and the guys all began scrambling because they'd promised Mr. Detmer they'd end at 1 A.M.

Now for the nicest part. Lew drove just me home. Of course, the backseat was filled with arms and legs and other gruesome tidbits, but that didn't matter. Nothing mattered besides the fact that just the two of us had our own space, our own world, our own us.

Friday, November 1

Life is so wonderful I resent having to waste time sleeping.

Saturday, November 2

Lew has gone to visit relatives for the weekend. In a way I resent that too, because between student government, every sport that was ever created, getting good grades, the school newspaper, etc., etc., etc., he has little time for me. I resent all of the above, but never—well, hardly ever—the time he spends with his mom. She was in what they call a state of MS remission for a while, but now she's getting worse fast.

I'm proud that Lew is good to her. He takes her on long walks in her wheelchair and carries her in and out to his car for church and special events, which she loves. He is really wonderful and considerate and patient, the way I'd always like to be, and most of the time am not.

Friday, November 22

I'm taking piano and flute lessons again and working hard at school and studying at home, and I'm trying to be as considerate and respectful of my mom as Lew is of his ... but ... I gotta admit I've got a way to go ... a lonnnnnnnng way. Aw ... come on, Self, give me a Brownie point or two for trying. I may not be good, but I am *better*—so there!

November 28—Thanksgiving—Blessed Thanksgiving!

Dad flew home to have Thanksgiving with Mom and me. We drove to Hilton Head and stayed at Dad's cousin's beach house. I felt like a little kid again, walking down the windy shore with Mom holding tightly to one hand and Dad holding tightly to the other. Sometimes we'd run away from each other and play hide-and-seek, sort of, in the tall rushes on the dunes. We'd stretch out flat on our stomachs or backs, and you could practically step on someone before you'd see them. Once Dad burrowed into the sand and Mom and I both looked until we each, in frustration, yelled, "I give up." Then Dad popped up right between us.

We ate dinner at our charming little lighthouse-looking place overlooking the pounding waves at Rocky Point. It was the kind of making-a-memory day that Thanksgiving was meant to be, ending up with us playing the old one-two-three, snap-your-fingers game. Only this time, instead of using states or cars or colors or girls' names, etc., we used things we were thankful for, and we played till the logs in the fireplace had turned to red embers. Even then we hadn't run out of things to be thankful for. Although we were sometimes getting down to mini-blessings like "liver" and "sea slugs" while we laughed and playfully hit on each other. Oh, I forgot to tell you. *I* got to do all the driving!

1:52 A.M.

I'm in the bathroom flushing the toilet so Mom and Dad won't hear me sob. About an hour ago Mom's muffled crying woke me up. I hurried into the bedroom and snuggled up next to her in bed. She whispered that she was "crying from complete happiness," but ... I DON'T THINK SO! Not with Dad sleeping up in the loft! I softly rubbed her shoulders and back like she has so often done mine when I needed her, and she soon fell asleep. Now *I'm* wide awake and wondering about ... everything.

Sunday, December 1

We took Dad to the airport, and we all cried. Only then did Mom and Dad hug each other like they really meant it. It was happy but sad too, because none of us wanted to break up. After a while, Dad hesitantly asked Mom if we'd both come to Phoenix for Christmas if he sent us tickets as early presents. Mom and I jumped up and down like she was part of the gaggle and said, "Yes, yes, yes," over and over again. Do you think possibly? ... maybe ... I'm afraid to hope ... but I do hope so anyway.

Saturday, December 21

Lew hurt both legs skiing. They had to bring him down the mountain on a snow cat. I wanted to be there with him, but of course that's impossible. He's in traction, so he'll have to stay with his uncle and aunt in Colorado for what will seem like forever to me. I wish I could do something more than just write.

Saturday, January 4

Dear Self:
I'm so sorry I haven't talked with you for so long, but I've been living in Heaven since Lew broke his right leg and hurt his left ankle. His mom asked me if I'd drive his car and take him to and from school, and it's turned into my being a full-time Lew-sitter. But I don't mind, oh, goodness no, I don't mind, in fact I insisted!!! I need to be needed. It's good for me! We're together from early morning every day until sometimes late at night. He's in a wheelchair, but he can lift himself, by upper-body strength, in and out of the car. I take him to the library and to all of his meetings and games and stuff. The maid takes his mom where she has to, or wants to, go. I'm as used to their house as mine and certainly getting acquainted with wheelchairs with both of them in what they call their "racing machines." Lew's isn't as fancy as his mom's. Hers runs on batteries, and she shifts it like a car. I think I'm good for her, and she and Lew are better than they'll ever know for me! I'm feeling better than I have felt in ages.

I hated to leave for the three days Mom and I went to Phoenix for Christmas, but Lew's brothers were there, so I'm sure they didn't miss me. Actually, I deeply hope that they did miss me a little . . . no, I want them to have missed me a *LOT!*

We had fun in Phoenix, putting up the tree in the patio by the pool and taking Mom over to Adam's so she could hear the Almost All Red Aborigines, etc. It was deeply hurtful when we had to leave. I know Mom and Dad still love each other in many ways, but Dad has pictures of Liz all over. I could see that pained Mom.

I missed the gaggle. They are like my sisters and *not* my brother. I wanted them to be with us, to do all the fun things there are to do in Phoenix, especially Dorie. She needs some new interests in her life. She's not the same since . . . you know. I wish I could do something . . . but we're all helpless to fill in that hole.

Lew's left leg is okay and his right one is in a walking cast, so he's back on his feet. He's happy, but I'm somber. It was *so* wonderful feeling needed, necessary, helpful, actually essential! I've never felt so . . . so . . . fulfilled in all my life. He's always telling me how much he loves me for what I did for him. Like I didn't *love* doing it? Like it didn't make me feel good?

Sunday, January 5

Life is still magnificent, glorious and heavenly, with just one horrible battering. The police called and said no one has been able to locate Collin. They wanted to come talk to me some more. I yelled, "NO, NO, NO," and broke down completely. I don't know what else they want me to tell them. I've dumped my whole load of gagging garbage. They seem to expect me to go back and wallow in it, wallow in it, wallow in it . . . for nothing. I won't! They can't make me! The police keep beating *me* down to a pulp while +-*&+_ continues out there unchecked, spreading his sunshine . . . well, *hardly* sunshine, more like death. But I won't think about that anymore. Come on, Scarlett, help me, help me think about it next never day.

Tuesday, January 14

Dearest dear Self:
Please, please tell me I'm wrong, but I know you can't. I'm beginning to run down again, aren't I? I can feel it like air being let out of a balloon. I'm trying so hard to eat right and to exercise and to rest and not let my emotions control me, but I can feel some unknowns slowly sucking the energy out of me like evil black, slimy, living things.

Oh, forget the above. I'm just being paranoid. I've got to snap out of it. YOU'VE GOT TO HELP ME, Self! I know you will and thanks. I've just got an attitude problem. Boo-hoo to me.

Wednesday, January 15

I am soooooo depressed. It's like I'm floundering in black quicksand. The world has slowed down to an ooze and has just lost its color and happy sounds. There is no way out, north, south, east, west, up or down. I can't! I *won't* let anybody see me like this!

Friday, January 17

Black, cold sleep is my only means of escape. Mom doesn't know it, but I've stopped eating altogether. Even Imperical's singing grates on my nerves. I've never felt like this before.

?_____

Mom picked me up bodily and forced me into Dr. Sheranian's clinic. Before, it seemed bright and yellow and white. Now it seems as black and gray and gloomy as everything else. His lightheartedness is like chalk grating on a blackboard, and I want outta here! One of the nurses gave me a shot which mellowed me out some, and then they started on the prodding, poking, sticking, checking routine again. Somewhere in the midst of it I passed out.

?_____

I'm here in the hospital AIDS ward, and I've made Mom promise everything she holds dear that she won't tell the gaggle. At this point their happiness and healthiness just make my blackness more black . . . I resent them! I almost hate them! Thought not nearly half as much as I resent and hate myself! I read somewhere once that people see the world and everything in it in direct ratio to how they see themselves. That *really* is true for me in my present state! I hope this ugly feeling doesn't last long. It's too brutally painful: physically, spiritually and mentally!!!!!! I hope I die soon. I really do.

?_____

Mom didn't want to lie for me, but I *made* her call the kids and tell them I'd gone to Dad's because *he* is sick again. He's *not* really sick, but then he probably is, though! *Sick of me* and all my physical and mental problems! Who in his right mind wouldn't be? Except Mom, of course; she's the biggest polyester, walk-on-me Pollyanna martyr of the world!

HELP me somebody, something! Part of me knows I'm acting and thinking totally irrationally, insisting on things that are neurotic and paranoid, but at this point in my abnormal life, wouldn't that kind of wacky, *abnormal behavior* be considered *normal?* I'm so confused and shut out . . . so lonely and unlovable, so worthless and lost. Oh please, please, God, let it be over; at least let me be feeling somewhat sane again, please, please, pretty please!

Tuesday, January 21

Mom has given in to my unreasonable schizo nagging and decided to let me go to Dad's. I can have home school there and lie around in the sun, then come back tan and healthy. I'm leaving tomorrow. I think she's glad to get rid of me!

Monday, January 27

Dad's

I can't believe how morbidly defeated I felt last week and how pretty good I feel now. It's almost like that black period happened to someone else. Still, Self, confidentially, in some little secret, hidden part of me, I still resent the kids a little because they're well and I'm not. It makes me feel ashamed and guilty and awful. Actually not fit to live even as long as I will.

Monday, February 3

Adam comes over nearly every afternoon or evening. We do lessons together, and he's brought the small electric piano. So sometimes we just fiddle around with our music. He's written a number of songs. Some of them are really good, haunting or happy or mainly beat, whatever he wants them to be. I'm *so* grateful for his friendship.

The gaggle sends me lots of letters and cards and stuff. I just mainly tell them lies. I hate it. Maybe it would be better if I didn't write, but then they would wonder. I can't tell them too much about Adam because Lew might get jealous or drop me, and I won't tell them *I* am the one who has been sick and that I'm having home school. . . . My life is such a mix-up. I wish I could just live *that* life when I'm *there* and *this* one when I'm *here*. Maybe I'll try. I won't answer the kids' letters. I'll tell them I'm too busy to write and that Dad needs the quiet, so they shouldn't phone. Ummm . . . what thinkest thou, oh, dear Shakespeare student, Self? Bad idea, huh? Sometimes I honestly think my mental processes are sicker than my body processes—*that* is really scary!

Tuesday, February 4

Went to see Dr. Marx again today, and he says I'm looking good. Then he pretended to cry and said *that* was awful because he needed the money I wouldn't be bringing in. He is soooo funny and kind and all the things people in his dreary profession should be. He says I'm free. Whee for me.

Wednesday, February 5

Guess I won't go home till Sunday because Adam has tickets to a concert Saturday. It seemed exciting before, but now I'm going only for him. Adam is such a special, priceless friend! I suspect he likes me a lot more, the other way, than I do him. Hope I never hurt him. I'd *never* hurt him consciously, ever, ever!

Saturday, February 8

7:02 A.M.

I just went to into the bathroom, and I'm bleeding a little. It's not like my period. Besides, I just finished that. I wish I had someone to talk to. I can't wait to call Dr. Marx. I'm so glad I know him. I'd be scared and embarrassed to death to go to someone I hadn't met before. It's going to be embarrassing enough to go to him. It kind of seems like I'm bleeding from my rectum, but that can't be ... can it? Oh, I hope he can see me before Monday. I can't wait until Monday. I really can't.

Twelve Noon

I called Dr. Marx's office at 8:30 A.M., and he was there. The nurse told me to come right in. I took the bus because I didn't want to worry Dad. He's working on plans for a huge building, and he's behind schedule. It's beautiful and it's using all new kinds of things ... and I'm trying to keep from telling you ... that ... *now* I have a rectal ulcer. It's AIDS-related, and I'm going to have to wear Depends *all* the time because blood ... you know ... all the old crap. Dr.

Marx wants me to come back Monday. Oh, *woe* is me. I read that somewhere once and thought it was funny. It's anything but that now. I *can't* go home tomorrow. I'm crushed. I called Adam. He'll take one of his buddies to the concert instead of me. Of course, I didn't tell him the true reason why I can't go.

Monday, February 10

10:30 A.M.

Dr. Marx insisted Dad come in with me at 8:30 A.M. He told us as gently as he could that he would suggest I stay in Phoenix, as the bleeding might suddenly get worse. We need to watch for complications for a while—and that I not even try to go back to regular school. It was like he was beating me with a club. Not go back home to my mother and my friends! Stay here and have a hermit school! It's not fair!

I went completely crazy and started screaming AND JUMPING UP AND DOWN and crying. I could hear and feel myself, but it was like somebody else had taken over. Dr. Marx gave me a shot to calm me down and prescribed some tranquilizers or something. I've just taken one, and I'm no longer climbing the ceiling of my cage, but I'M NOT *ME* ANYMORE. I don't think I ever will be.

Maybe the rectal ulcer will heal ... maybe I will be able to go back to a real school later ... maybe I won't have to wear diapers forever ... maybe my poor ego can eventually accept *this*

... may

be

...

6:30 P.M.

Dad and Liz have been out by the pool quarreling. I can't hear them, but I can tell by their body language. Liz called about noon to see how I was feeling. I told her "better," but I lied. I hope they aren't quarreling about me.

Later

A little while ago I tiptoed to the top of the stairs, and before Liz slammed out the front door, I heard her say how hurt she was that Dad hadn't been honest with her and how she *wouldn't* be in a relationship that wasn't honest. I feel so, so, so bad. It's all my fault. I probably should have stayed with Mom . . . or should I?

Everyone, including me, will be so much better off when I finally die. I wonder how soon it will be now. I'm going to call Dr. Marx in the morning and make him tell me; surely he knows, or at least has some idea. Then—depending upon the time—I can make plans for existence. I'm always *sooo* tired, and I'm down to 81 pounds.

Tuesday, February 11

11:32 P.M.

Dr. Marx sent over a Social Nurse or something early this morning. She told me how to handle my bed linen and stuff, being much more careful than before. Then I heard her out in the hall talking to Maria in Spanish. She'd brought a big box of rubber gloves and told Maria that she should always wear them when she was handling any of my personal soiled clothing and stuff. She tried to assure her that AIDS was not dangerous as long as she was careful, but I could hear the fear in Maria's voice as she asked again and again for reassurance.

Shortly after the nurse left, I saw Maria hurrying down the street, looking back at our house occasionally as though we or *it* was coming after her.

She left a note on the kitchen table telling Dad where to send her check.

Tuesday, February 25

12:40 P.M.

It's been two weeks since Maria left, and Dad can't get another maid to come near our house. Most of the women who do that kind of work in this area are Mexican, and I guess they have a gossip line like in every other town. Dad says we can take care of everything, but he has no idea. This is a biggggggg house, and I'm sure he hasn't done a dish or cleaned a tub since he's been here, till now. Besides, who is going to cook and shop and everything? I don't have the strength, even if Dad would let me . . . but he won't.

Wednesday, February 26

4:22 P.M.

Dad's been working nights and weekends, and it wasn't bad until Maria left. Now everything has piled up on us till we're being suffocated. The dishwasher's broken, and we've got ants that we can't get rid of. I'm trying really hard to not get my laundry mixed up with Dad's, but . . .

Thursday, February 27

10:02 A.M.

THIS IS NOT WORKING ... Dad doesn't deserve this! He doesn't deserve me! I don't deserve me!

I'm worried about the white mossy stuff in my mouth ... and sores. Dad's not safe around me. Dr. Marx keeps telling me he is, but ... I AM SOOO SCARED. My hair is brittle, breaking off and falling out in handfuls.

5:27 P.M.

Adam just called. We talk for hours on the phone each day. He is the only thing that saves my sanity. He's so worried about me and wants to come over, but I won't let him. I haven't told him that I have AIDS. I think he thinks it's mono ... that's bad enough ... but not this! My skin is shriveled as an old old lady's.

Friday, February 28

9:30 P.M.

I was feeling so lonely and alone. Then Mom flew in, and I fell completely apart. I wasn't even making sense as I poured out all the things I've been trying to keep from her for so long. I've been trying to just let her know the good things, but now she knows them all. She kept telling me everything would be all right, but I could hear the wetness and wonder in her voice, sloshing over her words.

She insists I go back with her as soon as she can get a flight. At first it sounded wonderful, but I can't go back *there!* I truly can't! Maybe I can just go to a hospice till ... you know. Dr. Marx suspects how I feel because he makes Dad dole out my pills so that I can't ... maybe I would ... maybe I wouldn't ... I'm a Catholic ... but I don't know. I'm sooo scary-looking and even more scary-feeling.

3:30 A.M.

Mom and I have talked all night. I guess I've never really realized how much I truly love her. After I'd convinced her that I absolutely can't stay with her, and I can't live here any longer, she had an awesome idea and called Aunt Thelma, in Idaho. I'll never forget going up there. It is like the Garden of Eden.

Aunt Thelma has a large ranch house with a little apartment on the back for her caretaker. It has everything modern, but it's made to look very rustic. Her caretaker, Melvin, has a twisted hand and foot on his left side, but he can still do everything any other man can do. He ropes the two horses they have and cuts wood and fixes fences and does everything including driving like a maniac over the dusty gravel roads. You can see him coming or going in a whirl of dust two miles away.

Some nights Aunt Thelma asks him to eat with her, and he tells funny or scary historic stories about pioneers and explorers and early settlers, or animals.

Mom told Aunt Thelma all the gory details about where I'm at now in my disease and how we'd be very far from a doctor who might want to help me in case we had a problem.

I went back and forth between being upset with her because she didn't tell enough, and being upset because she told too much. Oh, how I wished and prayed and hoped Aunt Thelma would let me come and stay there, at least till winter sets in, but it would be so wonderful and white there in the winter. It would be white-cloud heavenly to be there then.

Aunt Thelma said she'd need to think and pray about it, and she'd let us know in the morning. Aunt Thelma is a very religious lady. She says a prayer of thanksgiving in the morning and asks for help to get her through the day; then she says a prayer of thanks at night for all her blessings during the day. She also gives thanks for the food before each of her three meals. They are beautiful prayers, sort of like the Indians', always grateful, always positive, always loving and forgiving. I wish that everyone could feel like Aunt Thelma and the Indians.

4:49 A.M.

Mom and I went to bed, but I couldn't sleep, so I came down and read a magazine. It had an article in it about Haitian voodoo and how it really works if people believe in it, but most of the things were negatives. I was tempted to try it, but I think I'll stick to Aunt Thelma's kind of positive beliefs.

My eyes and body are sleepy, but my mind is as wide awake as at Christmas. I can't wait for Aunt Thelma to call back. Oh, please, please, please, Aunt Thelma, say yes. I know I'll be a nuisance and a bug, but I'll try awfully hard to not disrupt your lifestyle or anything. I honestly, truly will.

8:24 A.M.

The phone is ringing. It has to be Aunt Thelma saying yes!

10:41 A.M.

Aunt Thelma didn't call till a couple of minutes ago. I'd waited so long that I was sure it would be no . . . but it was *yes . . . yes . . . yes.* My heart is beating a hundred miles an hour. She said we'd try it for a couple of weeks and see how things worked out.

Oh, I will be so good and so kind and so helpful and so cheerful that she won't want me to ever leave until I . . . maybe then I can be buried under one of the big old trees like her husband, Uncle Rod, was. Aunt Thelma told Melvin about my having AIDS and said he didn't seem to mind either.

Mom says we can leave as soon as she can make the arrangements and have me see Dr. Marx so he can tell me what I should and shouldn't do to protect Aunt Thelma and Melvin. That in itself is a big responsibility because there is so much I wonder about. Like last week in the Phoenix newspaper there was an article about small-town police needing AIDS protective gear like firemen and EMTs have. I guess that's important because they don't know which victims have the HIV virus or hepatitis, and there are lots of bloody situations. I remember the police chief said something like "for lack of a better word, debris from self-inflicted gunshot wounds, or other situations . . . can be everywhere, and you don't know if the debris contains a disease that can take your life." I guess that's the space-people-looking stuff the people were wearing in the hospital when they cleaned up a room after the death of the AIDS patient—face shields, full-body disposable gowns, gloves, protective eyewear, etc.

I'll take everything Dr. Marx has for me to read and maybe he'll send me some stuff, or tell Dad where he can buy it and send it to me.

And I will always, every minute that I have rectal ulcers, wear Depends, even though it's a blow to my ego that is almost unbearable. I don't want to hurt anyone else, ever, except maybe Delta, who spread the awful rumor about my accident at the movie ... her I'd like to give AIDS to. No, no, dear God, I didn't mean that. Please forgive me. Please erase that thought. I NEED HELP. I NEED HELP.

How will dumb I ever know what to do and what not to do? Scary things are rattling around inside my skull. They're bouncing back and forth, banging against my eyeballs and eardrums and the top of my spinal cord.

Dad just walked into my room and for no reason, I started crying hysterically, completely out of control. It's not fair. I'm just a kid ... I'm just a kid. Dad hugged me so tightly and protectively and comfortingly and lovingly that I started to calm down, but I kept whispering over and over, "I only had sex once in my whole life. How did it happen? I'm just a kid ... it's not fair."

I blurted out all my plans too, after college and after I'd become a pediatrician, to get married and have children and then grandchildren, with Dad as the patriarch at all the reunions.

We were both crying on each other. He didn't know any more what to do or say than I did. Finally he just started saying, "I love you, I love you, I love you," over and over in small sobbing whispers, and finally I began saying it too. "I love you, I love you, I love you." It helped.

Tuesday, March 3

Aunt Thelma's

Dear Self:

I found you today, and I am *so* happy. I thought I'd lost you someplace between Dad's and here. I am soooooooo glad I didn't. From now on, you're going to be my only gaggle. Can two geese be a gaggle? I don't know about that, but I know two girls can be a gaggle. Right? Right! THAT'S US! This could get a little complicated if we'd let it, but we won't, right, no! I am not skitso. I am not a split personality. Oh, let's worry about that too next never day.

I'll catch you up. Aunt Thelma and Melvin met us at the toy airport with toy planes. It was really exciting. With Mom's luggage and mine and Mom and me and the pilot, we were squeezed in tight. Oh yes, he had a few big sacks full of wheat or potatoes or something for someone to pick up. Neither Mom nor I had ever been in a little prop plane, and it was like *Babes in Toyland.* Idaho is having a *very early spring* just for us!

We flew so low that we almost felt like we could reach out and pet the cows and horses and one little herd of deer we passed. The pilot saw a wolf and swerved the plane so he could chase it for a bit. I felt like part of a National Geographic expedition or something. Mom and I giggled and squealed. When the plane set down and I started to get out, my full skirt blew up. I hope everybody in the world couldn't see my fat, stuffed underpants. That's all I need. Everyone in the wide open spaces talking and speculating, here as well as there.

Gotta go, it's time for dinner. I wonder what we'll have, wild-bear steaks, poached possum or mountain oysters . . . that's a joke . . . you know what *they* are.

10:15 P.M.

I thought it would be quiet here at night, so quiet I could hear my heart beat, but it isn't: crickets are cricketing, frogs in the pond are croaking, birds in their nests are sleepily chirping, an occasional owl is hooting far away and I heard sundry other sounds. All of them are nice, comfortable, sleepy night sounds.

Aunt Thelma gave me the little upstairs room with one dormer window that comes down to the floor. I love it. I can see this whole side of the planet: mountain, sky, meadow, road, horse pasture, vegetable garden, fruit orchard, horse and cow barn, front lawn, pond, rose garden, old Red Alert, the dog moseying down the path to who knows where, and everything else of importance in this creation.

10:32 p.m.

I had to get up to tell you that the little single bed with a lace canopy has a feather *mattress!* Isn't that going to be cozy in the winter when it's cold outside? Don't worry, Mom put my rubber sheet over it so . . . you know . . .

Ummmm, I bet I'll be asleep before my head sinks into the pillow.

Friday, March 6

8:33 A.M.

Mom could only stay three days. She said she'd missed so much time she'd be hard put to pay the rent. When she saw my face, she laughed and reminded me of the big apartment house she'd sold a few months ago. That would tide her over for a long time.

We watched her little yellow plane take off and drift into the sky until it looked just like a butterfly. Then Aunt Thelma said we'd have to hurry home because she had some raspberry jam to make.

Saturday, March 7

10:14 P.M.

You know how I woke up this morning? It was like I was in coo-coo land, I was just lying there sleeping like a baby, and I had this real funny feeling on my chest, kind of soft and warm and semi-scary and weirdish. I began to open one eye just a sliver, and two big yellow, not human eyes were staring down into mine. I clamped my eye shut, thinking I'd been dreaming, but the soft weight was still spread out over my chest, and I could hear breathing and feel in-and-out air. I felt myself get as stiff as a board before I could peek out again. What if a wild animal had come in through my window? Just as I started to pull my head under the comforter, the animal started purring. It purred so loud I could feel the vibrations, and my eyes shot open in spite of myself.

Wow! What a monster cat! It tapped my cheek with its sheathed paw that felt big as a dog's paw.

Cautiously, I reached my hand out, and it rubbed its head back and forth against my fingers. Then, without an invitation, it tunneled down under the covers with me. We snuggled, it purring its heart out, and me purring my heart out too.

When I finally went down to breakfast, Aunt Thelma started laughing. "Oh, I see old Cougar's come home. He's been gone for three or four days. I guess he got hungry for cookies or something."

"He's not really a cougar, is he?" I whispered respectfully as he rubbed against my legs.

Aunt Thelma put her paintbrush down and came over and gave us both a hug. She told me that Cougar was just an old tomcat who had wandered up to the house so many years ago that it seemed like he'd been here always. She said he'd been hurt by some bigger animal, and for a long time neither Melvin nor she had thought he'd live. They had to shave most of his body to put splints on two broken legs and get the matted hair out of the big hole in his side, where whatever had taken a big bite out of him, literally. He was so sick they both wondered how he'd ever made it to the house. They fed him with an eye dropper, canned milk straight and vitamins and wheat germ and beaten-up eggs.

I was so engrossed in the story I almost asked, "Did he make it?" Even though I was sitting cross-legged on the floor, and he was sitting in my lap.

Aunt Thelma handed me Cougar's brush, and he loved being brushed as much as I loved doing it.

After a minute, Aunt Thelma went back to her painting, and I started for the kitchen.

Aunt Thelma called out after us, "His name is Cougar, because he sort of looks like one and because Melvin thinks it was a cougar that almost did him in."

I reached down and hugged my new, very best friend in the world. He reached over and took a soft little playful bite on my cheek. He knew! I knew he knew how much I needed him. Not that he'll ever take the place of you, dear Self, but now we're three—isn't that positively smart?

I called back to Aunt Thelma, "How often does he run away?"

I guess she heard the anxiety in my voice, because she laughingly told me that he didn't do it often, maybe a couple of times a year. Ordinarily he just followed along behind the dog, but *he* wasn't friendly. Melvin had trained him to be a watchdog and protect the animals. Oh, Self, aren't you glad, glad, glad we've got Cougar?

Sunday, March 8

5 A.M.

My new world is just beginning to get a good head start on the day. Samuel the Lamanite (the giant rooster, and king of the barnyard) is standing on the wall outside the chicken coop, crowing like the fowl alarm clock he is. I guess maybe some mornings I'll spell that "foul," but today I'm glad he woke me and Cougar up. We don't want to miss a second of the day. I wonder why they call him Samuel the Lamanite; that's such a funny name. Sometime I'll ask Aunt Thelma or Melvin.

Aunt Thelma said Cougar and I can go anywhere that Red Alert will go with us. I hope he's not a lazy stay-at-home dog, because I want Cougar to show me all the secret, special places on our whole mountain. I'll fix a lunch of the goodies they both like every time we go, so that maybe they'll want to go often, even when they don't really want to go.

10:22 A.M.

Melvin has dug a big, deep trench behind the chicken house. It's so that I can throw my used Depends and stuff away. He's put a chicken wire fence around it with a gate so that Red Alert and other animals won't get at them and ... I don't know ... I don't think animals can get AIDS—actually, I know they can't ... I think! That's another question I want to ask; although I think I know the answer is no. Anyway, this way we'll all be sure. We have flush toilets and a septic tank, so I feel pretty secure about not giving *it* to anyone or anything else. That would truly be more than I could bear ... so I not only won't think about it tomorrow, I just won't think about it at all, ever!

12:30 A.M.

At first, Red Alert, part wolf, part lazy dog, didn't want to move off his mat under the shade of the big old tree outside Aunt Thelma's dining room window, but I'd suspected that, so I held out one of his dog treats. He grumbled and slobbered and lollygagged over to get it. I gave it to him and walked a few feet away and held out another one. After about five he had his motor warmed up and seemed happy to take me up the path toward the little Indian Paint Brush waterfall.

It was so beautiful and wonderful. There was a little meadow of sprouting mustard beneath it, and the fragrance was like nothing else in the world, not sweet like flowers, just clean and fresh and natural-smelling. Maybe someday I'll bring the big sack of letters the gaggle has written me up there, and I'll sit in the shade by a big rock and become part of them (the letters, I mean). I haven't been able to let the kids back into my life until now ... but maybe ... maybe not.

7:04 P.M.

I'm loving it here like no one back home could imagine. I feel so close to nature and to God. This afternoon Aunt Thelma and Melvin dressed up in their very Sunday best. Melvin even wore a suit. I wouldn't have believed he had one! We bounced along over the gravel roads for an hour and a half to get to the little Ward Church house. It's really different from the Catholic service, which is all formal and repetitious. It's just kind of friendly and old-fashioned, with kids on the program and women.

At dusk Melvin started teaching me to drive his gear-shift old truck with no power steering. Thelma was having fits because I sometimes started looking at something and got off the road into the brush. I'll be glad when I can drive the truck by myself. I'll go as fast as the machine can go, mostly off the roads, and the dust clouds will be so big they'll become one with the ones in the sky.

Back to church. I know as a Catholic I shouldn't feel comfortable there, but I do. It's my belief and Lew's that GOD COMES WHEREVER LOVE IS.

10:10 A.M.

Melvin has a guitar, and he's teaching me to play three songs. Church songs. They make me feel good. They are: "Where Love Is, There God Is Also" and "I Am a Child of God" and "Love at Home." Maybe that's not church—but if it isn't, it should be. Melvin is going to teach me some country songs after I memorize the chords for these. That's funny, because Aunt Thelma listens mostly to classical music. I myself sometimes take my Ghetto Blaster and go up above the falls and turn it on as loud as it will go and listen to kid music. Red Alert covers his ears and whines or slithers away, but he never goes far. Melvin threatened to make him into dog stew if he didn't take good care of me and Cougar.

Cougar is the funniest cat I've ever seen. He follows me and Red Alert anywhere, even when we climb on the steep rocks by the little falls. Aunt Thelma says the stream only runs heavy enough for it to be a waterfall all year when they have a good snowpack up above. Thank goodness they did last winter, because it's the most sacredly beautiful place in the world.

Another funny, nice thing about Aunt Thelma is she thanks God for everything under the sun all the time. I like that. It's showing appreciation and caring. I'm trying hard to be more like that. Nearly every day she paints in her studio or out around the ranch; then twice a year she takes her works to art shows and sells them. It's an ideal way to live, and she makes good money doing what she loves doing and would do for nothing if she had to. I hope I have a profession like that. I dream of being a pediatrician, so I guess *that* fits into the category. But . . . sometimes I forget about my future or my no-future . . . I pray somebody will soon find a cure. Oh, I really, truly, honestly do.

Thursday, March 12

5:10 A.M.

Aunt Thelma came in and woke me and Cougar up. She says she has a surprise for me . . . I wonder what it can be. Guess I better hurry and get dressed so I can find out. . . . See ya.

7:30 P.M.

When I got downstairs, Melvin had both Sonny and Cher saddled up with big fat backpacks on both of them. Thank goodness I was wearing my jeans, and more thank goodnesses that baggies are in.

Anyway, I climbed up on Cher a little timidly. I'd only been on two horses before in my life. Once at the pony ride when I was little and once up at El's uncle's cabin. Aunt Thelma jumped up on Sonny like a real cowboy, or "cowperson" or whatever, and we started up the trail with Red Alert following us. Oh yes, Melvin had strapped a basket in front of me on the saddle to put Cougar in. Cougar didn't seem to mind. In fact, he just curled up and went back to sleep like it was nothing.

As we took off, Melvin hollered that Sonny started out leading and that after a while Cher would take over, but not to worry—she knew where she was going. If she didn't, Aunt Thelma would giddy-up Sonny to lead.

It's been a soft spring, dozens of shades of new green, a day always to remember. We crossed the stream with the horses kind of picking, slipping over the rocks. I was scared and reached over Cougar and held on to the saddle horn for dear life, but Cougar didn't seem to mind it at all. In the middle of the water, Cher stopped to get a drink, and I thought I was going to slide down over her head, but the saddle stayed steady. On the other side, she stooped down to nibble at wild clover with little popping-out purple pom-poms on top. Aunt Thelma told me to pull up her head and kick her in the flanks, but I didn't dare. I didn't want to take ANY chance of falling off and having to go to the hospital or something. Far away, in a place I'd never seen before, we stopped in a just-beginning-to-leaf, dense aspen grove. Before we got there a few wildflowers were so high, they brushed against the horses' bellies, and fragrances you wouldn't believe lightly spumed up around us, except when Sonny, in front of us, pooped or let gas, which was *often!*

When we stopped, Aunt Thelma brought out her paint stuff and a lunch box that would have served a tribe of Indians if they had swooped down on us from the rocks above.

Cougar was slinking around curiously, checking things out, and Red Alert was down the hill barking and chasing a rabbit or a squirrel or something. Aunt Thelma said she hoped it wasn't a skunk, that he'd done *that* a couple of times and gotten sprayed.

Aunt Thelma set up two collapsible willow easels that Melvin had made for her, and she asked me to look on her right and tell her what I saw. I just saw some chunks of reddish rough rocks that looked like

197

they'd rolled down the mountain when the Earth was created.

Aunt Thelma laughed and told me that was an interesting observation, but that I hadn't *REALLY* looked for the things that only the eye of appreciation could see.

I walked closer. It was still a pile of rocks.

"Look closer," she whispered.

I did, and snuggled down in between the big rocks was a miniature garden with teensy, teensy flowers smaller and more fragile-looking than any I had ever seen. She brought out a magnifying glass, and we examined each leaf pattern and stem and petal as well as their dimensional relationship to the rest of the flower. The flowers were like ... well ... I felt like I did the last time I was here. That I was Gulliver in *Gulliver's Travels*. It was the neatest experience. Us giants and *them* normal.

After a bit, Aunt Thelma had me close my eyes and describe the picture of the tiny garden in the minutest detail. I remembered she'd done that before when I had been here. This time she had me study the little, lovely garden three times, then *verbally* paint a picture of it for her as though she were blind. I really wanted to do a good job and tried very hard, finding it challenging but fascinating too.

Aunt Thelma and I then started mixing paints, first white, then a little red, then a bare touch of blue and a speck of yellow. Finally she had *almost* the *exact* color of the blossoms. She easily mixed colors for the stem and leaves and rocks, and we began painting. Cougar curled up in his basket by my feet and in the distance the horses whinnied, and the bees buzzed and the butterflies floated, and life was perfect, absolutely perfect! Who needed a radio? The music of nature was enough.

Occasionally Aunt Thelma would reach over and put a little dab here or there on my painting, or tell me I was using too much paint or too little or had a wrong brush stroke or something. She was doing a big canvas, and I was doing a small one that would practically have the flowers at their real size.

We'd stop occasionally and go for a little walk or lie down and just listen and love and be a part of life, plus every little while Aunt Thelma and I and Cougar and Red Alert would have a little snack. Once Red Alert ran away. I could hear him far, far away in the distance. I got concerned, but Aunt Thelma said, "He's probably gone back to the stream for a drink." She didn't suspect he liked lemonade.

The day passed much too quickly, and I didn't think about . . . you know . . . even once.

When I'd finished my picture, Aunt Thelma pulled out the picture I'd painted the first time I was here. This one was a million times better than that one, but Aunt Thelma's was a million, million times better than mine.

Melvin had made special frames for the paintings so the paint wouldn't smear, and obviously Sonny was used to carrying the big floppy canvases, one on each flank.

I wish every day for the rest of my life could be so . . . so . . . there are not positive enough words to describe it, except . . . maybe *sacred?*

11:20 P.M.

I try to stay so busy that I can't think, but I don't know how I can stay so busy that I forget to talk to you, dear Self, but I really do. Melvin's teaching me to play the guitar, and we're going to get a guitar book when we go to town, and then he's going to teach me to read music and to *write* my own songs. I want to write one about the ranch and everything around it. I wonder if any words or music could ever express the beauty that is here. Aunt Thelma is teaching me to paint, as you know, and with me helping Melvin with the chickens and the cows and the horses and Ballard, the crippled mallard duck that lives with the chickens (he thinks he's one of them), and canning and drying and weeding (I don't do much of that—it's too hard). Anyway, I'm positively, always positively pooped.

Sunday, March 15

Mom and Dad came up for the weekend. I almost wish they hadn't. IT H-U-R-T-S sooooooooooo much when they leave! I've a bushel of letters from the gaggle and Adam. I can't read them, and I wish they wouldn't phone and phone and phone! It makes life too *real!* It's not! I'm not! Sometimes I wish they'd all just leave me alone ... BUT I'M GLAD THEY DON'T TOO! I don't know what I wish. I wish I did.

Monday, March 16

4:30 A.M.

Last night a bronchial problem flared up. I really got concerned ... actually, I got scared spitless ... then a strange thing happened. Cougar, who had been sleeping at the foot of the bed like he does usually, came up beside me and started purring and licking my cheek. It helped me calm down and almost go back to sleep. Then it happened again, and I felt like I couldn't breathe. For a second I thought that would be a good way to go and I tried to relax, but I couldn't. It hurt too much and felt too evil. I started whimpering softly, not wanting to wake Aunt Thelma, but not being able to control the sounds either.

After a second or two, I heard Red Alert softly scratching on the front door. He's allowed to come into the house anytime he wants, but he doesn't seem to want to very often. I let him in, and he followed me right up to my bed and popped in on the side opposite Cougar. His big, hairy, part-wolf, part-German-shepherd body took up most of the room in my single bed, but I felt good and cuddled and safe in there. For a moment I wasn't sure that Aunt Thelma would like his outside body on her inside homemade quilt comforter, but *that* wasn't the most important thing in my life at that moment.

Red Alert made a soft little deep, growling sound like, "Now I'm here to take care of you, go back to sleep and don't bug me." He yawned, and his monstrous teeth and his huge big mouth in his huge head made me mind him.

Wednesday, March 18

8:27 P.M.

I've felt miserable the last couple of days. Like I've got a terrible case of the flu, but I can't let Aunt Thelma see it! I try to do everything I usually do and appear upbeat and perky, but inside I'm ANYTHING BUT THAT . . . OH, it is *sooooo* bad. Red Alert has been sleeping on my bed every night. I put a sheet over the comforter so Aunt Thelma won't know, but I feel guilty about that too. Red Alert isn't out where he can protect everything else, and I'd feel awful if a weasel or a skunk or something got in and killed Ballard or any of the others.

Red Alert takes up so much room that sometimes I can hardly turn over, or when I do I find my head in his hair or his face. And much as I love him, he does have *DOG BREATH*. IN FACT, I've seen him eat doo-doo, and if he's in the house he drinks out of the toilet. Who wants a friend who does that? *I do!*

Thursday, March 19

9:21 A.M.

Aunt Thelma and Melvin are worried about me. They think I'm depressed, but I'm *not!* I'm as filled with bubbly sunshine as I was when I first got here. It's just that I have no energy, *none at all!* It makes me tired to eat, and I *have* to eat so I won't hurt Aunt Thelma's feelings as well as to keep up what little strength I have.

Aunt Thelma finally asked me what I thought we should do. The only thing I could think of was to call Dr. Sheranian in South Carolina. He probably knows as much as anyone about AIDS. At least he's supposed to, and I trust him. I hope he tells me it will go away or that I can take some medicine or something.

10:01 A.M.

We've got a call in for Dr. S. now. The nurse said he'd probably call during his lunch break if he didn't have an emergency. Let's see, one hour and 59 minutes. I guess I can wait that long.

I don't feel like it, but I'm going out to the clover patch and try to find a lucky four-leaf clover.

Oh, before I go, let me tell you about cagey Red Alert. Every morning early, he whines softly or breathes in my face till his breath wakes me up; then I let him out before Aunt Thelma wakes up. Before I get back in bed, I fold up the sheet and tuck it under the mattress. It's great now, but I wonder what's going to happen when it rains, or during the winter when he's covered with slush snow. Oh well, we'll face that battlefield when we come to it.

1:40 P.M.

Dr. Sheranian called back at 12:33. Melvin was on the porch working, and Aunt Thelma was sitting at the kitchen table so at least she would hear my side of the conversation. Red Alert was sitting at her feet, and Cougar was sitting at mine. First Dr. S. told me how much he loved me and missed me and how he wishes we could just be friends instead of doctor and patient; then he listened patiently to everything I had to say. I was embarrassed to talk about some of the stuff in front of Aunt Thelma, but I told him every detail anyway, about how the rectal ulcer flared up and went down and how I still sometimes wet the bed, although I tried to drink a lot in the morning and little in the afternoon and evening; and about my mouth and eyes and now my hurty chest and my lack of energy.

He asked me if my chest felt like it had when I'd had pneumonia, and I said no, it was just like all my insides were swelling and getting stuffed up. He waited for a minute, then reminded me that we had once talked about death. It had seemed ugly and cruel and mean then, but it didn't seem so much that way now. After a while, he suggested I just slow down for a week or so and then call him back, sooner if anything big happened.

I FELT SOOOOOOOO RELIEVED. I'd thought maybe he'd suggest I go to some hospital somewhere . . . but he said no, to stay here. Isn't that wonderful! Aren't you happy out of your skin? Aunt Thelma and Melvin and I all danced around the room like three nutso school's-out kids.

Friday, March 20

5:30 A.M.

First day of *real spring!* Maybe I'll have a reawakening too! I hope! I was going to sleep in this morning, but Samuel the Lamanite stood on his wall and cock-a-doodle-dooed till he woke me up.

I appreciate so much that Aunt Thelma and Melvin don't try to coddle or overprotect or baby me. They know I'm trying to listen to my body and stay cool. The only time they got uptight was when a big fat rattlesnake slithered out just in front of me when I was going to take my plastic bag of personal garbage to the trench where I put it in and then shovel a little dirt in on it so the flies and stuff wouldn't come there. Old Red Alert was there and had that snake's neck in his mouth before I let out my first scream. I was so afraid that he'd get bitten that I wanted to go in and help him, but I didn't know what end of which one I should try to grab, or if I should run for the shovel.

By the time Aunt Thelma and Melvin got there, I was a wimpy, shaking pile of Jell-O. In fact, Melvin had to practically carry me into the house. He would have completely carried me if Aunt Thelma hadn't given him a stern look. She wanted me to stay as independent as I could. Like she wouldn't wash my bedding, nor would she let Melvin do it. I'm sure she would, though, if I really needed it. She even took the box of rubber gloves that I had put inside on my bedroom table out in the hall and put it in the linen closet.

Sunday, March 22

1:32 P.M.

I told Aunt Thelma that she and Melvin should go to church, that I'd be all right at the ranch with Red Alert to protect me, but she smiled and said they'd decided to have church at home. I didn't know you could do that, except I remember Red's uncle Bill had.

It was really special. Melvin said the opening prayer, and we all three sang my favorite songs with Aunt Thelma on the piano and me accompanying on the guitar and Melvin playing his mandolin. "Love at Home," "Where Love Is, There God Is Also," and "I Am a Child of God," my very favorite favorites.

Aunt Thelma talked about LOVING GOD AND LOVING OUR NEIGHBOR AS OURSELVES, and then Melvin talked about DO UNTO OTHERS AS YOU WOULD HAVE THEM DO UNTO YOU. He said that all major churches have that Golden Rule in common. That made me super happy.

It was a strange feeling, though, when Aunt Thelma asked me to say the closing prayer. I wanted not to . . . but I wanted to too, so I stumbled through all the thanksgivings I could think of, and there were plenty. In fact, I'd just gotten a good start when Aunt Thelma coughed politely, and I said, "Amen." It felt good. It was the best church service we've ever been to. Didn't you think so, Self?

2:10 P.M.

Dear Self:
This seems really crazy, crackers, nutso, bananas, but as I feel worse in the physical me, I seem to be feeling stronger and brighter and lighter in the spiritual me. Does that make sense? No, I didn't think so . . . but it's still the way I feel. And I don't feel so *all-the-time hollow-lonely anymore for everyone.* THAT'S weird too, isn't it?

9:30 P.M.

This afternoon, Aunt Thelma called a lady she thinks I would like to know. She's going to fly up in a few days on our puddle jumper. Aunt Thelma won't tell me who it is, but she says it's going to be a VERY SPECIAL, WONDERFUL surprise! Who could it be? Hmmm—my mom, no. She would have told me. Dad . . . no, he's not a woman. . . . I guess I'll just have to wait and see.

Black Monday, March 23

Today the most tragic thing in my life happened. Red Alert didn't come in for his breakfast, and it seemed especially quiet around the place. Melvin and Aunt Thelma and I all went looking for him. He's always around for meals. After we'd looked every place we could think of, even on my bed, we looked in his dogaloo, which has a door on it that opens and closes when he gets close to it, like a garage door, except the electric thing is on his collar and works automatically.

Anyway, he was all curled up in there, and we thought he was asleep, but he was dead. Melvin said he'd died peacefully in his sleep. It really, honestly looked like that is what had happened, because he almost had a smile on his face.

At first I felt almost heartbroken; then Aunt Thelma explained to me about what a wonderful life he'd had here at the ranch and that he was lucky to go in such a kind way.

You know, I've been thinking about it, and I suspect that all the time he was comforting me when I was sick, I was comforting him too, because he was sick and just couldn't tell us. Do you think that's possible?

3:30 P.M.

Aunt Thelma made me rest while she and Melvin built Red Alert a nice coffin. She lined it with one of her beautiful handmade baby quilts and covered him with a lovely white lace curtain. Melvin cleaned and brushed his fur.

It was an awesome funeral. We sang "Where Love Is," changing the words to "Where God is, there Red Alert is also. Where God is, I want to be," etc. Then Melvin played his guitar and sang a couple of good-bye songs. Only Aunt Thelma and Melvin and God and Cougar and I were there, and it was very sacred!

Melvin had dug a big place for Red Alert's coffin just down aways from Uncle Rod's grave. He'd lined it with soft grasses and flower petals. Red Alert was just like he was asleep when Melvin put the cover on and more wildflowers over it. Aunt Thelma read about how much Jesus loved animals as well as people.

I know Red Alert is in Heaven! It just wouldn't be Heaven without *him* there!

Aunt Thelma said he would have been over one hundred years old in dog years. Can you imagine that? And he still did all the dog chores on the ranch, every one of them. In fact, no one can take his place, ever. Melvin said that. Aunt Thelma told God that he always did his chores "with the proper attitude and a happy heart." I wish I could be like that. Isn't it funny, me saying I'd like to be like a dog?

I hope we won't ever have to get another dog, but then, I guess we have to. We can't have a ranch without a dog.

?_____

I don't know what time it is, but Aunt Thelma just sneaked into my room and woke me up. She had called a friend whose dog had had puppies by Red Alert many years ago. That lady had given one of his pups to her daughter, who had given one of his pups to her granddaughter, and it had just had puppies a few months back. They still had a little male that Aunt Thelma could have.

I sat up in bed so fast that lights flashed off and on in my head when Aunt Thelma told me that we are going to get one of Red Alert's great-grandsons. I asked Aunt Thelma if we could name him RA4. She thought that would be nice. Now I'm going to sleep dreaming about RA4 and his great-grandpa up in

Heaven. I wonder if Red Alert knows about RA4. I hope he does!

?_____

I woke up dreaming that I was down in the box with Red Alert. It was black and heavy and suffocating. I don't understand death. I don't want to die! Aunt Thelma says the body stays here and the spirit goes back up to Heaven. That I'd like. In fact, some days when I feel so miserable, I'm almost looking forward to being gone from my body . . . but then I'm not, too. I've been thinking about Mom and Dad. I try not to because it makes me too lonesome and hungry for them. They come up here as often as they can, but they're very busy, and it costs a lot of money, and it's *sooooooooooo* hard on me when they go.

When I woke up I was mumbling, "Mama, Mama, Mama," in my sleep. "Come get me, Mama." But there is no way she could take care of me. Not now, with her working and all. I guess life is as it should be.

Tuesday, March 24

Melvin brought home the new dog. I thought he'd be a real puppy, but he's almost as big as Red Alert, and he's as cautious about us as we are about him.

Melvin has a muzzle on him because he is part wolf, and he's been taught to be aggressive. He growled, and his eyes got red, like Red Alert's when I came close. It really hurt my feelings, because I thought he'd taken Red Alert's place, but then, I guess one person never can take another person's place completely. Right? Right!

Oh well, I still have old Cougar. Melvin says he'll have to teach them to be friends, at least civil to each other.

Wednesday, March 25

7:22 A.M.

I spend a lot of time just sitting on the steps in the sun these days. I do a little schoolwork, but Aunt Thelma says I don't have to push till I feel better. Melvin brings in lots of magazines and letters and the week-old newspapers when he goes to town. The newspapers are funny because we've seen almost everything they say on the news already. I feel like I'm a psychic that I can tell them what's going to happen. The gaggle and Adam all write regularly, but they seem almost like people in the news or magazines or something now, not quite real.

I try not to think about them. It hurts too much. My dear, loving Mom and Dad come often, but I can't allow myself to think about them either; that just shrivels and shreds and pulverizes me. It makes me feel like an ugly, hopeless, mortally suffering, displaced person who doesn't belong anywhere. I *must* detach myself! I must live only for the *here*—the *now!* It's the only way *I* can handle my life at this point.

3 P.M.

WOW! WOWIE! WOWERS! Wonders never cease! Mom and Dad came in on the puddle jumper about 9:30 and then Melvin drove in with El about noon. WHAT A WONDERFUL, HAPPY, MAGNIFICENT, MORE-THAN-PERFECT DAY! I'm so filled with love and joy and gratitude that I feel like all 72 pounds of me is going to explode with such magnitude that I'll cover the entire earth with happy little sunshine pieces. Mom made me come up to my room to rest, but I can't. I want to jump up and down and squeal and giggle. Mom and Dad almost never let go of each other's hands. I hope with all my heart that means what I hope it means. And El, dear, precious, forever friend El, she got her parents to give her a trip here instead of a birthday party and presents and stuff. Isn't that beyond fantastic?

4:29 P.M.

I just woke up from a little nap. In a way I hate to leave my cozy, warm, loved-filled room. El brought me big poster-size, blowup pictures of each of the gaggle, and they are covering my walls.

5:33 P.M.

While my loved ones and I were outside on chaise lounges by the duck pond, El and Melvin put a grinning life-size poster of Lew on the ceiling. I love it! But even more I love the small, serious picture of him that El put on my nightstand. He had carefully written across the bottom of it, "Nancy, I shall love you through all time and infinity, and I'm coming up as soon as school is out."

My heart is leaping within me. Life is good.

Sunday, March 29

I'm soooo lonely. Mom and Dad and El all had to leave at noon to catch their planes. I hurt so much I can hardly breathe. I can't understand how inside your heart pains can hurt even more than outside pains. I guess I've just *got to detach myself* from my *out-there* life! Please, God, help me! Honestly, I can't stand this!

3:10 P.M.

Guess what? God heard my prayer and answered it through RA4. A while ago I went down to the lounge Melvin had put out for me by the pond, and when I woke up from a little nap, RA4 was lying by my side. I was so excited I felt my pounding heart would wake him up, but it didn't.

When I moved, he woke up and smiled at me, and when I touched him, he kissed my hand. I guess he senses how much I need him *now!* He's the real master of the ranch and keeps everything in line except Cougar. When he starts coming Cougar's way, even accidentally, Cougar just stands his ground and puts up his fur and hisses, with one unsheathed claw in the air. I'd be respectful too. His claw looks about a foot long. Oh, thank you, RA4, for filling in the hole in my life.

?_____

For the last few days, since everyone went home, time has stopped dead in its tracks.

I think it's Monday, April 6

Oh yes, it is, because tomorrow my surprise is coming. Why would I *like* a stranger lady? I mean ... I don't know what I mean.

Tuesday, April 7

Oh, Self:

I've had the most lovely day. Mr. Pederson brought Aunt Thelma's friend in on the helicopter, which he only does on very special occasions. They landed in the meadow down by the pond, scaring the living daylights out of the wild ducks. It was funny and fun seeing them all go up as the helicopter came down, quacking in a multicolored cloud and flapping crazily in every which direction.

I can't believe that the lady was Dr. B., who put together one of my favorite books, *Go Ask Alice,* from the diary of a girl my age who had gotten into drugs.

As soon as Aunt Thelma introduced us and told me about Dr. B.., I knew what they were thinking immediately! A light as big as those strobe lights that shoot up in the sky for new store openings popped on in my brain. Ever since I first found out I had AIDS, I've wished, like everything, that I had someone to talk to about it, someone who could answer my questions or at least question *my* answers. After a few minutes, Aunt Thelma excused herself and went up to the house, leaving me and Dr. B. to talk about . . . *my book!!!* It seemed unreal, but Dr. B. assured me it was *as real a possibility as I was.*

I felt like we had been friends forever, like we were long-lost relatives or something. She said Aunt Thelma had called her and said it might be good for me to unload my pain and strain with someone who was knowledgeable . . . and that . . . anyway, she's here and I'm glad, I'm *really* glad! Maybe I can do something in some way to help other kids who are in my situation. I really hope so. I'm still not sure if I was raped, or if I just set myself up for it, but I guess I'll never know *that* answer for sure. *I do know* that I shouldn't have had a boy over when Mom was gone and that I shouldn't have gotten drunk. It was really my first time . . . except that New Year's Eve with Red. Oh, crap, I am so tired of beating myself up. If I'd known then what I know now, would I have acted more sensibly? Crazy thoughts, go away . . . go away . . . if you must come again, come next *never day!*

2:07 P.M.

Aunt Thelma suggested I rest after lunch, which we had down by the pond. It was really nice.

But I can't rest. I'm too excited. I feel more excited and healthy and strong than I have in, I can't remember when. Maybe this will make me get well. Being happy and feeling helpful and all like that might bring up my immune system and my endorphins and all that self-healing stuff. Oh, I do hope so . . . miracles do happen! *This* might be a miracle! Oh, please, please let it be a miracle, God.

Dr. B. has worked with troubled kids for many years—drugs, alcohol and all the other stuff. I told her about my junior high and how filthy lots of the kids talked and how immoral a lot of them were . . . but I didn't tell her about Dorie. She's different. She just got carried away and let her hormones take over her brain. Anyway, Dr. B. said she understood what I was saying, but that kids had to learn that they "couldn't keep birds from flying over their heads, but they could keep them from making nests in their hair." I like that! If I don't . . . you know . . . pretty soon, I think maybe I'll be a writer. There would certainly be plenty of stuff to write about up here. All

Melvin's stories, and about Aunt Thelma and Uncle Rod and how they came up here many years ago after he had a stroke, and his face was all kind of funny and weird. Originally, they were going to stay here just for a while. He'd write his column, and she'd paint, and they'd move back to New York when he recovered, but he never did recover, and they never did want to leave, and then he died.

I can't wait any longer. I've got to go down. I guess writing would be considered the same as resting, right?

Say Right!
Okay. Right!

10:30 P.M.

Tomorrow morning Melvin is going to hitch up an old buggy that hasn't been used in years, and Aunt Thelma is going to take Dr. B. and me up to some of the places I love. She'll bring her painting gear and go off and paint somewhere so Dr. B. and I can be alone. She's *so* thoughtful! I know she knows there are some things and feelings I want to pretend she doesn't know. Like it's sooooooooooo hard on me to have her have to wear all the protective gear she has to wear when she gives me a bath and changes my bed and stuff. At first she didn't want to do it, but I insisted because Dr. Sheranian said she *must!* She's always got scratches and blisters from working in the garden and helping Melvin with fences and stuff. Anyway, that hurts a lot, especially when my rectal ulcers flare up and there are little pools of blood. I almost panic! It's sooooooo gross, even with my diapers. *No* teenage kid should have to wear diapers—especially me! No—especially anybody!

But I've got to think about positive things, like what we're going to do tomorrow.

I've been famished all day. The first time in forever that food has really tasted good. Aunt Thelma even put some raisin oatmeal cookies and milk on my nightstand, and I've eaten three of them, can you believe that? And a half a glass of milk. I guess some of the reason I haven't eaten much for a while is because, with the rectal ulcer, when I go BM, it's like fire-and-brimstone-type hell literally; even my urine on them is like salt on an open wound. IT *IS* SALT ON AN OPEN WOUND. But I've *got* to eat so I can get better, don't I? "The lesser of two evils," as someone once said.

OH, SELF, TURN THAT GARBAGE OFF ... RELAX ... THINK OF TOMORROW ... EXACTLY WHERE WILL WE GO? What do I want to ask Dr. B. and to tell her? Actually ... I better go to sleep so I'll have some energy, right? Right!

Friday, April 10

5:20 A.M.

I can hear Aunt Thelma stirring around downstairs, trying to get things ready so she can come up and help me, but I feel so good I can do it all by myself.

5:49 A.M.

I started to go downstairs, filled with excitement about the day. *Then* I passed the full-length mirror at the top of the stairs. The sun was shining in on it, and the creature that looked back at me was like something from a horror flick! Stringy hair! Whatever happened to my beautiful blond hair? Sunken eyes and big ugly black things starting on my face and neck. Suddenly, I don't want to go anywhere. I want to lock myself in my room and never, NEVER, NEVER COME OUT!

But that's stupid. Dr. B. and I have to finish my book to help other kids! *That* will be my legacy. I will never have children to live after me . . . to make a difference in the world . . .

Aunt Thelma and Melvin's motto is "DO IT." So, Self, finish with your Pity Party and let's get moving. Don't pay any attention to that lying old mirror in the hall. Close your eyes when you walk past it and think of yourself as pretty as you used to be.

7:59 P.M.

I have never been so exhausted in my life, Self, but it's a good exhaustion because we've had a day fit for the gods. Aunt Thelma took food enough for an army and three folding lounges so we could take a couple of naps during the day. At least Cougar and I did. I think maybe Aunt Thelma read, and Dr. B went over her notes and tapes.

We went up to Indian Paint Brush Falls and over to the aspen grove and down by the foot of the mountain in the little fir tree circle where Uncle Rod and Red Alert are buried. Dr. B. called it a Sacred Circle, and I think she's right. I will from now on think of it as that too.

We talked about death for a long time, like it was a friend, and great streaks of noonday light shone straight down from Heaven and engulfed and caressed us. Did that sound goony? *It really was true!*

217

And if I'm going to be a writer, I have to learn to *think* in true detail like Aunt Thelma taught me to do with my painting.

Dr. B. believes as Aunt Thelma does, that when I die, my spirit, which isn't actually sick at all, will just waft up through a tunnel of light, like people who have had near-death experiences say. Dr. B. says she's also heard of many people who have had loved ones come to escort them; she calls Heaven "home." I like that too! And it really will be HOME with my little brother, who died when he was two days old, and Grandma Ivy and Great-Grandpa John, and Catsup and Cougar and Uncle Rod, etc. I hope Uncle Rod is sent to take me "HOME." Why did I write Cougar? I meant Red Alert, but I think Cougar will be going "home" soon too.

RA4 has become a constant companion when I'm outside, but he'll never be Red Alert, and there could never possibly, worlds without end, be another Cougar. Maybe there shouldn't be. I hope there's never another ME, except ME.

EPILOGUE

Nancy died in her sleep April 12th—two days after her last entry.

She is buried next to Uncle Rod in the center of the Sacred Fir Tree Circle. Red Alert's grave is close to Nancy's feet, and ailing Cougar will be buried beside him.

On Nancy's wooden tombstone Melvin carved:

THERE WILL NEVER BE ANOTHER NANCY

Questions Nancy Wanted Answered About Rape and AIDS

1. Will I ever recover from being raped?

Emphatically *yes!* If you talk to a rape counselor and learn to know truly that YOU WERE NOT RESPONSIBLE! That if you said no, it should have meant no! That you were a victim! That you are not alone! That thousands of others before you have recovered! That *you will also!*

2. What should anyone, boy or girl, do after he or she is raped?

Get to a phone as soon as possible. Call 911, the police or your local Rape Crisis Center. They will get you to a hospital or clinic. DO NOT BATHE, WASH, CHANGE CLOTHES, GO TO THE BATHROOM, DRINK ANYTHING OR BRUSH YOUR TEETH.

3. Why?

Because semen is as identifiable as fingerprints and there may be a trace in your mouth as well as on your clothes, etc.

4. Will going to a hospital immediately after you are raped keep you from becoming pregnant or getting AIDS or other diseases?

The nurse or doctor at your local hospital or clinic will give you medications to prevent pregnancy. They will also use antibiotics for STD (sexually transmitted diseases). However, AIDS and Herpes II virus cannot, at this time, be controlled by ANY MEDICATIONS.

5. Are most rapists scary strangers in the bushes?

No; 72 percent of reported rapes are acquaintance rapes (meaning family members, friends, neighbors, etc.) or date rapes. Only 22 percent are stranger rapes. Professionals in the field estimate that over 80 percent of rapes are *not* reported. Very few boys report rapes or call hot lines, although they should. (Source: National Victim's Center, Arlington, VA 22201.)

6. *Where can someone go to see if he or she has been infected with the AIDS virus? How much does it cost?*

Call your local, city, county or state health department to find out where and when you can take the test. The tests are usually confidential and sometimes free.

7. *How long does it take?*

It usually takes from two to three weeks before you will know your test results. Often retesting is suggested as it sometimes takes longer to become antibody positive. In rare cases it may take up to a year. DURING THAT TIME, IF INFECTED, YOU ARE CONTAGIOUS.

8. *What is HIV?*

When you become HIV positive, it means you have the HUMAN IMMUNO-DEFICIENCY VIRUS in your body. It is the first stage of AIDS, and is contagious. Anyone, male or female, can infect a sexual partner IMMEDIATELY after acquiring HIV from a sexual encounter with an HIV-infected person. IN OTHER WORDS, IF ONE HAS SEXUAL CONTACT WITH AN HIV-INFECTED PERSON ON FRIDAY NIGHT, AND BECOMES INFECTED, HE OR SHE CAN PASS THAT INFECTION ON TO SOMEONE ELSE ON SATURDAY—OR EVEN LATER THAT SAME DAY!

9. *What is AIDS?*

It is the second stage of HIV infection. AIDS

means "Acquired Immune Deficiency Syndrome." It is a disease you can be infected with. It is not an illness people are born with, like hemophilia.

"Immune Deficiency" means that the AIDS virus causes your body's immune system to break down. HIV is a tiny virus or germ that has to live inside a living cell. (See chart on page 229.) When the virus invades your body, it breaks into the cells that are part of your immune system and turns the infected cells into virus factories, cloning out copies in such great numbers that they attack and conquer other cells that are key parts of your immune system. You then are open to all diseases, including rare ones that would not affect you if you were in normal health. As time passes, your body becomes less and less able to fight off infections and diseases.

10. How do you feel when you have AIDS?

Many of the AIDS symptoms are like those of the flu—night sweats, fevers, a cough, shortness of breath, etc. You may have swollen glands for long periods—in your neck, under your arms or in your groin. You may have constant diarrhea or lose your appetite, feel tired and run-down, have rashes that persist, and white patches or sores in your mouth. If you have Kaposi's sarcoma, you will have patches or bumplike bruises on parts of your body.

11. Is AIDS really epidemic? ("prevalent and spreading rapidly" —Webster)

Yes. AIDS, since 1981, when it was discovered, has been growing almost unchecked. Across the United States hundreds of people die daily of AIDS; two or three times as many find out they are infected; *many more go around not knowing they are infected!*

People infected with AIDS live in every state and in most countries.

A study from the U.S. Federal Centers for Disease Control and Prevention was presented at the 1993 International Conference on AIDS. It suggests that sex educators need to stress the message that *pregnancy prevention* and *disease prevention* are not the same thing.

More than 12,000 high school students, 54% of whom were sexually active, were surveyed. Among this group, 52% had not used condoms the last time they had sex. Those who had had more than four partners, or who used drugs or alcohol, "sometimes used condoms." Only 19% of the 18% who relied on birth control pills used condoms regularly.

Dr. Victoria Cargill of Case Western Reserve University reported that many kids say, "Why am I going to use a condom for some disease you don't even get for ten years?" Researcher Janet Collins suggests that "once an adolescent is protected against pregnancy, the motivation to use condoms seems to be reduced."

Kristine Gebbie, America's new AIDS coordinator, and the thousands of other scientists who met at the annual international conference on AIDS repeatedly emphasized that *prevention* is the only way to stop the AIDS epidemic from continuing to spread widely and rapidly throughout the world, and that at this point AIDS prevention is an *individual responsibility,* with the exception of cases of rape, such as Nancy's.

12. Will everyone who has AIDS die?

Today, as far as professionals know, AIDS is always fatal. Most people with it die within two years of their HIV having advanced to AIDS diagnosis;

however, infected people react differently. Some test positive for HIV but go on for years without symptoms. Some people who are infected get very sick right away and die within a short time. Others drift back and forth between health and sickness.

13. What about blood transfusions?

Blood is carefully screened today, tested several times to make sure it is not contaminated with the AIDS virus. If you *GIVE BLOOD,* the blood bank uses a brand-new needle for every donor. There is no way you can pick up the AIDS virus there.

For Vaccinations doctors also use a new needle and a new throwaway syringe for each patient and for each inoculation.

14. Can you become infected with the AIDS virus the first time you have sex?

Absolutely, if your partner has the virus and does not use protection, or if the protection is ineffective. You can also get pregnant from having sex just once under the same circumstances. Most people in their twenties who have AIDS became infected with HIV when they were in their teens.

15. How safe is "safe sex"?

Not 100 percent. Even using a latex condom with a spermicide is not 100 percent safe 100 percent of the time.

16. What is considered safe sex?

Obviously, not having sex is absolutely safe sex. So is sex with one faithful, long-term partner who is not HIV positive. If you are having sex with more than one partner, if your partner is infected or if you aren't sure about his/her back ground, you MUST use condoms during sex—oral, anal or vaginal.

Invasion Period

The virus invades the body. You may have no symptoms or you may develop a severe flu-like illness, with high fevers, sweats, rashes and fatigue. These symptoms, or others, can occur anytime after you become infected with the HIV virus and can last for a few days to a few weeks. *But you are contagious.*

Laboratory tests for HIV antibodies is negative. *But you are contagious.*

Time: From infection to development of antibodies is usually from six *weeks* to three *months*. Some people may take up to one year to develop antibodies. *During this time you can infect others.*

Incubation Period

The virus is inactive—no symptoms. *The person is infected and can infect others.*

Time: Includes invasion period from infection to symptoms. Can be from five to ten *years*.

AIDS

A sober assessment about the lack of substantial progress against the AIDS epidemic was sounded repeatedly in Berlin when thousands of scientists met at the annual International Conference on AIDS.

How the AIDS Virus Attacks

1. Everyone has T cells, a protective type of white blood cell.

2. Your immune system is constantly producing new T cells or antibodies. They destroy the germs or viruses you are exposed to every day.

3. When you have been infected with the HIV virus it begins destroying your T cells.

4. As the HIV-AIDS virus multiplies, it does more and more damage to your infection-fighting T cells.

5. When T cells are destroyed, your immune system can no longer attack and destroy disease-producing microorganisms.

6. You no longer have resistance against life-threatening infections.

Condoms can be bought in most drugstores. You don't need a doctor's prescription. Some drugstores and discount chains have sections marked "Prophylactics" or "Family Planning," so you don't have to ask for them.

Always use latex condoms with a spermicide containing nonoxynol-9. Condoms made of animal skin can be penetrated by the AIDS virus.

New York City has 20 percent of all cases reported in the United States. Condoms are distributed in public high school clinics there in an effort to curb the AIDS disease.

17. How safe are condoms?

The medical field considers condoms "unreliable barriers" against pregnancy. Condoms can break or leak if they are old or if they have been exposed to heat. Check the expiration date on each package. Always keep condoms at room temperature, not in a wallet or glove compartment. Do not buy unsealed condoms, and do not reuse them. Never use petroleum jelly or any other lubricant with an oil in it along with a condom. It may cause the condom to break. Instead use K-Y jelly, a water-based lubricant. THE FDA CRITERIA FOR CONDOMS SPECIFY THAT "IN ANY GIVEN BATCH, THE WATER LEAKAGE CANNOT EXCEED FOUR CONDOMS PER THOUSAND" (from *Condoms for Prevention of Sexually Transmitted Diseases,* sponsored by the American Social Health Association, Family Health International).

18. What happens after you get AIDS?

Most people who are HIV positive or have full-blown AIDS take medicines every day for various reasons. None of the drugs can cure AIDS, but doctors feel the earlier you start taking medication, the better your chances are of living longer. AZT is one of the most-often-used drugs. It was developed as a cancer drug but did not work there; however, it does slow reproduction of the AIDS virus in the body.

Unfortunately, AZT has some negative side effects. It can damage bone marrow, leading to anemia, and it also irritates muscles. Sometimes the side effects are so bad that people choose not to take it. DDI and ddC are drugs that are sometimes used in place of AZT or in combination with AZT, although they too can have severe side effects. Petamidine, as well as a number of other drugs, is used to treat and prevent pneumocystis pneumonia, but unhappily there is, at this time, no known cure for AIDS. (Studies presented at the International AIDS Conference questioned the effectiveness of AZT. The American Centers for Disease Control chooses to continue with research regarding that drug as well as others.)

19. How long before there is a cure for AIDS?
Scientists are currently working on over 40 different drugs. A few tests are even bypassing the animal-testing methods usually used for new drugs. *One problem with finding a cure for AIDS is that the AIDS virus is constantly changing and adapting itself to new conditions, including drugs.*

An AIDS vaccine, like a vaccine against smallpox or polio, is being worked on. A vaccine is a weakened or killed form of the virus that is the cause of a particular disease. When a healthy person is given a vaccine shot, his or her immune system develops antibodies that protect him or her from the weakened virus. Later, if the person is exposed to that particular virus, the antibodies will shield him or her from the disease. In 1992 the U.S. Government spent $4.383 billion on AIDS. In 1993 it spent $4.971 billion, plus $200 million on a Ryan White package, making it over $5 billion.

20. How can you catch AIDS?

AIDS it not airborne. The AIDS virus lives in human blood, semen or vaginal secretions. It is not a fragile virus. Outside the human body, it can survive in small amounts of blood in hypodermic needles or syringes for up to seven days.

Nearly always, one person catches AIDS from another by doing certain things that let an infected person's blood or bodily fluids into his or her own bloodstream. This can happen if you have sex with an infected person without using a condom (preferably latex with a spermicide containing nonoxynol-9). You can also get AIDS if you use a hypodermic needle without sterilizing the needle first. Your risk is high if you share a needle to shoot drugs, get tattooed, have steroid injections, acupuncture treatments, or your ears pierced by a careless person.

Having unprotected sex with a stranger, or anyone you don't know well, or with several partners is also extremely dangerous. Even if only one of the partners is infected, he or she could well pass it on to you, and you could infect others unknowingly.

It is also risky to combine drinking or drug use with sex, because alcohol and drugs impair your reactions and long-range reasoning abilities, and you might possibly lose your head and forget or momentarily not care.

If an HIV-infected man has unprotected sex, or uses "protection" that does not work, with a man or a woman, he can transmit the virus to him or her.

Through the same kind of unsafe or ineffectively protected sex, a woman can infect men and other women.

21. What about AIDS babies?

If a woman is infected with HIV and becomes pregnant, there is about a 30 percent chance that the baby will be born with the virus. Today thousands of babies are born HIV positive and will later develop AIDS. They could become infected before, during or soon after birth. A mother who is HIV positive and breast-feeds her baby could pass on the virus through her milk. HIV-positive women should not become pregnant or try to nurse.

22. Wouldn't Norplant be good for HIV-infected women? Exactly how do they work?

Yes. The Norplant is composed of miniature strips implanted in a woman's upper arm. It will keep her from becoming pregnant for up to five years. The Norplant is a minor procedure which can be done by a nurse in a few minutes. It keeps a woman from becoming pregnant but in no way protects her from getting or giving AIDS.

A school in Baltimore has introduced a Norplant pilot program in hopes of curtailing their uncontrolled teen pregnancy problem.

23. What can an HIV-infected person do if he or she gets cut?

Advice to an HIV-infected person is always, "Take responsibility for your own blood." Be sure to put the tissue, paper towel, etc., in a sealed plastic bag inside another plastic bag. People working with an AIDS patient's blood always wear gloves and sometimes a

Blood-to-Blood
Transmission

Riskiest Behaviors

- Sharing drug works
  (including steroids and antibiotics)

- Sharing tattoo equipment

- Sharing ANY skin-piercing
  equipment (earrings, nose rings,
  belly rings, etc.)

Co-Factors to Infection

- Drug abuse

- *Poor health!*

- Repeated exposures

How can I get AIDS?

You can get HIV-AIDS if you have any unprotected or ineffectively protected sexual, or blood-to-blood, experience with an HIV/AIDS-infected person. You are now capable of passing the HIV-AIDS virus on to the next person you contact sexually or in a blood-to-blood experience.

Invasion Period: How long before I know if I have AIDS?

It may be six to twelve weeks before the HIV-AIDS virus shows up in an AIDS test, but you nonetheless are infectious and capable of passing it on to the next person you contact sexually or in a blood-to-blood fashion. Some people are infected and fail to test positive for up to one year.

How long before I go from HIV (the first stage of AIDS) to AIDS?

After you are infected with the HIV-AIDS virus, you may go from five to ten years without few or no symptoms, or your body's T cells, which are your infection-fighting cells, may begin to break down shortly after you are infected. During this time you are infected and contagious.

What happens when I get full-blown AIDS?

Today, as far as professionals know, AIDS is always fatal. The majority of people with it die within two years of their HIV HAVING ADVANCED TO AN AIDS diagnosis.

mask, gown, cap and goggles if there is any chance of the blood splashing.

Schools and public places are required by law to have proper disposal for possibly infected waste: AIDS, hepatitis B, etc.

24. What does an HIV-infected person do with used tampons?

Flush them where possible. If not possible, put them in a plastic bag within another plastic bag.

25. What does an HIV-infected person do if he or she has an open pimple?

Be safe. Take self-responsibility. Wash hands carefully with soap and water, perhaps cover the pimple with a Band-Aid.

26. What about an HIV-infected person kissing if he or she has bleeding gums?

Again, be self-responsible. Think of others. Give them the benefit of the doubt. *IF YOU DOUBT, DON'T!* Be careful about not using anyone else's toothbrush.

27. What about used pads when you have rectal ulcers?

It is so sad to see a young boy have to wear Kotex pads because of rectal ulcers, but an HIV-infected person must, and must dispose of them carefully in double plastic bags.

28. What about urine, like when I wet my pants in the movie?

Very rarely would there be a problem in a situation like that. For bed-wetting, use heavy disinfectants like Purex when washing wet bedding. If there is blood in your urine, treat the urine as though it were blood.

Sexual
Transmission

Condoms are not 100 percent safe.
Spermicides are not 100 percent safe.

Used together, they are not
100 percent safe 100 percent of the time.

Riskiest Behaviors

- Unprotected anal sex
- Unprotected vaginal sex
- Sexual fluids on open sores on skin
- Multiple partners of unknown HIV status
- Oral sex

Co-Factors to Infection

- Genital sores; mouth sores
- Drug abuse
- Poor health
- Repeated exposures

29. Can animals get AIDS from people? Can people get AIDS from animals?

No, you cannot give AIDS to your dog, Red Alert, nor to your cat, Cougar, by sleeping with them and loving them. AIDS cannot be transmitted from insect or animal bites.

30. How could I give AIDS to someone?

You cannot transmit it by any kind of casual contact: shaking hands, holding hands, hugging, coughing, sneezing, eating utensils, toilet seats, doorknobs, etc.

Studies have never shown the AIDS virus to be transmitted during any kind of kissing, but tiny amounts of the virus have been found in an infected person's saliva, so you may want to be careful, especially if you have sores in your mouth or bleeding gums.

31. How will Aunt Thelma clean my room ... when I ... you know ...?

She will wear gloves and possibly a gown and disinfect it carefully. You need not worry about anyone else using the room. Everyone will love it as you do. Actually, they'll love it even more because *you* were there.

HIV IS NOT TRANSMITTED BY CASUAL CONTACT

Shaking Hands

Hugging

Kissing
(Unless one has open sores or bleeding gums)

Coughing, Sneezing

Eating Utensils

Toilet Seats

Doorknobs, Telephones

Swimming Pools

Insect or Animal Bites

RESOURCES

The answers were supplied by:
- Rape Center, National Victim's Center, Arlington, VA 22201
- National AIDS Hotline, Association for the Care of Children (Pediatric AIDS) Bethesda, MD
- Foundation for Children with AIDS, Roxbury, MA
- National AIDS Clearing House
- TAP, Teen AIDS Program
- Planned Parenting, Adolescent Education
- Family Health Service National
- Children with HIV Infections and Their Families
- U.S. National Disease Center in Atlanta CDC, FDA, WHO (World Health Organization), etc.
- Division of Public Health Service Budgets

Free 800 numbers to call for answers regarding HIV, AIDS and Support Systems:
- National AIDS Clearing House (1-800-458-5231)
- CHAPS—Children's Hospital AIDS Program (1-800-362-0071)
- TAP—Teen AIDS Program (1-800-234-TEEN)
- National AIDS Hotline (1-800-342-2437)
- Spanish (1-800-344-7432)
- Deaf access (1-800-243-7889)

These hotlines are staffed with information specialists who can offer a wide variety of written materials and answers regarding any HIV-infection or AIDS questions you may have.

Thanks to all of the above plus Margie Golden with the Department of Health and Human Services; Leslie from the Rape Crisis Center; Nancy's doctors; Nancy's mom and dad, Aunt Thelma, Melvin and many others.